"Brooks, do you take Melissa to be your lawful wedded wife? To have and to hold . . ."

The words seemed dreamlike. Melissa wasn't sure how they had gotten there so fast, but she was ready. She looked at Brooks. She wanted to smile, but her mouth was trembling. Instead, she squeezed his hand and waited for his answer.

"Uh . . ." was all he said.

"Brooks, do you take Melissa to be your lawful wedded wife? To have and to hold . . ." the minister repeated.

Brooks was sweating heavily now. He let go of her hand and took a step away.

Melissa realized that something was wrong. The minister had closed the pages of the book.

"Brooks," she said quietly. "Brooks?"

Don't miss these books
in the exciting FRESHMAN DORM series

FRESHMAN WEDDING

LINDA A. COONEY

HarperPaperbacks
A Division of HarperCollins*Publishers*

HarperPaperbacks   *A Division of* HarperCollins*Publishers*
10 East 53rd Street, New York, N.Y. 10022

Cover illustration by Tony Greco

First printing: June 1992

Printed in the United States of America

HarperPaperbacks and colophon are trademarks of HarperCollins*Publishers*

❖ 10 9 8 7 6 5 4 3 2 1

FRESHMAN WEDDING

One

"Melissa, I think we took a wrong turn."

"No we didn't, Brooks."

"It's no big deal, Mel. Let's just go back and ask directions."

Directions? Melissa didn't want to stop for directions. She was scared that if they turned the car engine off, they'd never get started again—they'd never reach their destination.

"We don't need directions! I know where we are," she insisted.

"Mel, it's dark. This isn't some kind of track meet you have to win. We're just lost."

"We're not lost, Brooks. We simply haven't gotten there yet!"

Brooks didn't react to Melissa's shouting. Instead he kept his eyes on the road, his hands on the wheel. He steered the car so that it followed the path of the headlights along the dark country road. Melissa turned to look at him. The fighting, the silence, and the uncertainty of whether they were doing the right thing was making her increasingly edgy. But somehow Brooks still looked patient, cheerful, confident, and together.

"I'm sorry," Melissa apologized. "I'm just jumpy."

Brooks shrugged, as if being sorry were another everyday occurrence.

"Well, I *am* sorry!" Melissa repeated.

"I know. It's okay." Brooks leaned forward and cleaned the windshield with his cuff. His golden hair and yellow windbreaker reflected the moonlight in the car's dark interior.

Melissa took a deep breath. She was wearing a U of S warm-up suit over clean running tights and a jersey. Her red hair was held back with a headband. She hadn't had time to change into anything fancier since they'd rushed off campus immediately after her track meet—a meet she'd lost, as a matter of fact, but for once losing hadn't seemed quite so important.

"Look, Mel, let's just stop and see if we can figure out where we are on the map," Brooks said. "How about that?" They were looking for some unknown house in some unknown little town, hours from Springfield.

Melissa folded her arms. "Fine."

They pulled over next to a grove of trees. On the other side of the street was a small white farmhouse with a buzzing bug light and a screened-in porch.

Brooks looked over the map, his tanned forehead wrinkling up. "I guess we're not off to a very good start," he admitted.

"Tell me about it," Melissa accused. "You're completely lost."

"I'm not talking about the drive, Mel. What I mean is, this isn't exactly a great start for the beginning of the rest of our lives."

Melissa shrugged and stuck her track shoes on the dashboard. "I guess not," she said, resting her chin on her fists.

Brooks put the map down on his lap. "Look, why are we fighting?" he asked. "What's going on here? Mel, is there something you want to tell me? Do you want to call this off?"

Melissa's heart did a triple jump, but she

didn't move. In fact she barely breathed. "Do *you* want to call it off?" she whispered.

Brooks's expression was somewhere between knowing and not knowing, between being confused and certain. It was an expression Melissa knew well—because she had been wearing the same one for the last few weeks. "We could just go back to the dorms and forget this whole thing," Brooks suggested without conviction. "We could find Faith and Winnie and the rest of our friends and tell them we changed our minds."

"Brooks, it's after midnight," Melissa pointed out. "I don't think Faith and Winnie are waiting up for us back at the dorms."

"It was just a suggestion, Mel," Brooks answered. "Why are you so mad at me?"

"I'm not mad at you!"

Brooks banged the steering wheel. "Well, everything I do sure drives you crazy. Sometimes *I* don't know why you want to get married at all!"

Melissa curled up, trying to calm the violent thudding inside her chest. Finally he'd said the word: M.A.R.R.I.A.G.E. They'd decided to get married several weeks ago, and now they were suddenly eloping. The purpose of their drive was to find a justice of the peace named Robert J. Schlosser. He was the man who would tie the knot.

"You know, we don't have to get married."

"I thought you wanted to get married."

Brooks sighed. "I thought we *both* wanted to."

Melissa began to tremble. She did want to marry Brooks, even though she wasn't in the mood to admit it. Brooks was her anchor, her rock. She came from a family where people screamed and screwed up, while Brooks was steadfast and focused and calm. Sure, she was a top freshman runner and premed on scholarship, but sometimes she was scared of her own shadow. Straight-arrow Brooks never seemed scared of anything.

"Mel, I only wanted to elope because you didn't want a big wedding."

"I know," she muttered.

Actually Melissa really had wanted a big wedding. The problem was that her parents couldn't afford it to pay for one, and she wasn't about to accept charity from Brooks's parents. That's when Brooks had brought up the idea of eloping, which had sounded so unpredictable, so *un*-Brooks-like, that it had made Melissa wonder if he'd wandered into some brain-transplant experiment at the university medical school.

Melissa finally raised her face and really looked at him. As she took in his square jaw, his earnest blue eyes, and sturdy, athletic body, she was suddenly overwhelmed by the reason she'd agreed to marry him in the first place. She loved him. Deeply. Totally. More than she'd thought she could love anyone.

Brooks moved closer. "Mel, please tell me what's wrong," he whispered. "I love you. Whatever it is, we can work it out. Believe me."

Melissa leaned into him without even meaning to. She breathed in his warmth and his strength and wondered if the trouble was precisely that she didn't believe. Maybe she was too scared to believe that they would work everything out. Maybe she didn't believe that someone as wonderful as Brooks would really love her for the rest of her life.

Brooks pushed stray hairs off her forehead, then kissed her cheek. "Mel, talk to me," he said softly. "Tell me what's wrong."

"I'm just scared, I guess," she finally admitted. Simply saying the words had caused a sob to press against her throat. She nestled even closer to him and rested her face against his chest.

"I'm scared, too."

A tear rolled down Melissa's face, and then another. "You?"

Brooks nodded. "Me."

"I thought nothing intimidated you," she challenged. "Not honors' college, not climbing mountains or rafting white water or finals or anything."

He pulled back to look at her again. "That was before I met Melissa McDormand."

She managed a smile. For a long time they just stared into each other's eyes. She started to feel more sure, more breathless and heady with each second that passed.

Then he smiled, too, and rested his forehead against hers. "Come on," he said, pausing to kiss her mouth. "Let's at least walk over to that farmhouse and ask them where we are." He nudged her. "I'll even admit that you're going to marry a guy who has no sense of direction."

Melissa laughed and reached for the door handle. She got out and quickly went around to open Brooks's door. "Right," she scoffed, pulling him out of the car, then slipping her arms around his waist. "No sense of direction at all," she joked, knowing that every time she had tried to take their relationship off course, he'd been the one to steer them back on again.

Brooks smiled and took her in his arms. They both stood very still until he kissed her—a long, slow kiss that made her reel.

"Let's go," Brooks said, when they broke apart.

Hand in hand they walked across the dark road. Soon they went up a brick path and onto the screened in porch. Then at the same moment they both read the sign on the farm-house door.

ROBERT J. SCHLOSSER, JUSTICE OF THE PEACE.

"I don't believe it!" Brooks howled. "This is it."

"See!" Melissa shrieked. "I told you I knew where we were."

Brooks tickled her. "Yeah, sure, you're clairvoyant."

"I did know," she insisted, laughing. "This proves that you should always trust me."

"I do trust you." Suddenly he stopped laughing. His eyes were deadly serious. They both grew quiet. "It's just that a lot of the time you don't trust me."

Before Melissa could start another argument,

the door swung open and another porch light flickered on. Even though it was late, the man who appeared was dressed in corduroy pants and an oxford shirt and bow tie. He also had bifocals halfway down his nose.

"I'm Judge Schlosser," he volunteered. "How can I help you?"

Brooks hesitated, but only for a moment. "I'm Brooks Baldwin," he said, stepping forward with an enthusiastic handshake. "Soon to be Brooks McDormand-Baldwin. And this is Melissa McDormand, soon to be Melissa Baldwin-McDormand."

Melissa began to giggle. She and Brooks had fought royally about what names they would use after they were married. Brooks had assumed that she would use only Baldwin. She'd fought that one, and won.

The judge looked confused.

"We'd like to get married," Brooks said.

"Oh yes. Oh, of course," the judge stammered. "Well, welcome. Come in, come in." He led them past the front door and into a study off the living room. The smell of freshly baked pie wafted in from the kitchen, and the sound of an old movie could be heard coming from a back room.

The judge's study was small but full of leather-bound books and curios. His diploma from law school, his certificates of acknowledgment from the state bar association, and other official documents hung on one wall. The sight of it all made Melissa begin to tremble again.

Brooks clasped his hand tightly around hers.

The judge gave them a warm smile. "Let's get the dull part over with first," he said. "Then I can lecture you about commitment and responsibility and all those things I love to go on and on about."

Melissa looked at Brooks. Her heart was pounding again and her head was light. This was it. It was really going to happen. Right now. She'd never be single, alone, or plain old Melissa McDormand again.

The judge pushed some papers around his desk. "First, I need your marriage license."

Everything stopped. As if they'd gone into slow motion, Melissa looked at Brooks. He looked back at her. They both looked at the judge.

"License?" she peeped.

"License?" Brooks echoed.

Judge Schlosser leaned forward and took off his glasses. "You forgot the license?"

They both nodded.

The judge let out a heavy sigh, then rubbed his beard. "There's no wedding without a license. But I'll tell you what," he said as he stood up. "You can both stay here tonight and get the license first thing in the morning. That'll give you a little time to think things over."

Judge Schlosser's eyes changed. Melissa guessed that he had noticed that they weren't exactly dressed for a wedding. "You know, marriage isn't something to rush into," he advised. "Especially at your age."

"We know," Brooks blurted.

The judge raised his hands. "I just mean that you don't want to get married on an impulse. You don't want to do it because you're running away from problems. You want to get married because you're absolutely sure, without any doubt, that you want to share the ups and downs of your life with another person."

Before Melissa could pick a fight with him, the judge was halfway out the door. "I'll go tell my wife to get your rooms ready," he said, puttering down the hall toward the sound of the television.

Melissa looked at Brooks, who was staring out past his folded hands. "What are you thinking, Brooks?" she prompted.

Brooks got up and looked out into the dark night. "*Are* we rushing into this?"

Melissa looked down at her running tights and shoes. She took the headband out of her hair and thought about the judge's reference to "running away." Maybe that's why she'd won an athletic scholarship. Running fast came so naturally to her. "What do you think?" she whispered.

"I want to get married only once," Brooks said, turning to look at her "And for me this is it."

"Only once for me, too," Melissa said.

"Then I think we should do it." Brooks paused. "I mean, if you think eloping is right, then it's okay with me. I just want both of us to be sure."

Melissa had never been sure of anything. And she was growing less sure by the second. All the wonderful images she'd been too afraid to think about flooded her brain: a beautiful, long, white dress; Faith and Winnie as bridesmaids; flowers; music; a bouquet; all of her friends and family witnessing the fact that someone actually loved her enough to pledge himself to her for the rest of his life. And not just someone—Brooks Baldwin.

At the same time she felt such a deep wave of

terror that she almost couldn't speak. Her mouth went dry. Her brain felt fuzzy. She took a deep breath and struggled until she finally found her voice. "Would your parents still pay for a big wedding if we changed our minds?"

Brooks's eyes brightened. "Are you kidding! My mother would jump for joy." He moved closer, putting his arms around her neck and his face next to hers. "Oh Mel, do you really want to pull out all the stops?"

Melissa pressed close to him. She suddenly knew that she had to stop running and fighting and worrying about who won and who lost. If she and Brooks were going to make it, it was time for her to *trust*.

"Yes," she said. "We'll tell the judge we're going back to Springfield. Then we'll call your folks and start planning the wedding of the century."

Brooks swept her off the floor and spun her around so hard that they almost knocked over the judge's chair. "God, I love you."

"I love *you* so much," Melissa cried.

"It'll be better this way, Mel," Brooks said. "Everyone who's special to us will be there. Our wedding will be perfect. You'll see!"

For the first time Melissa felt as if she really did see. Maybe, just maybe, this would really work out. Brooks made her feel like it could happen. Brooks made her feel like there were all kinds of possibilities.

And Brooks kept kissing her, even when they heard the judge coming back down the hall.

Two

·····················

"Josh, can you believe all this stuff? What are we going to do with it?"

"Since I fell in love with you, Winnie, I can believe anything: flying saucers, Elvis being alive and living in my computer, love at twelfth sight—"

Winnie kissed him. "I must be that kind of girl."

Kimberly Dayton laughed. "Seriously, you two. There's some pretty good loot here. A very homey teapot from Faith. A potted plant from me. A copper saucepan." She lifted up the pan and examined it. "Wow! This was expensive. Should we just return all these wedding-shower gifts?"

Winnie didn't know. She and Josh Gaffey sat entwined on her dorm-room floor while tall Kimberly was stretched out in a position that only an ex–dance major could find comfortable. Winnie's usual mountain of dirty clothes, study notes, and candy wrappers had been replaced by a sheet cake and wedding shower presents intended for Brooks and her roommate, Melissa. The food and gifts had been sitting on the floor since the previous evening.

Kimberly retaped the bottom of a gift-wrapped box. "Do you think we should have opened Melissa and Brooks's presents?"

"We didn't really open them," Winnie corrected. She looped a piece of gold-and-white ribbon around Josh's head. "We just sneaked a few peeks. A few major peeks."

"Well, I think it's definitely against the rules of every wedding-shower handbook," Josh cracked. The ribbon had gotten hung up on his single earring, so he tugged it down over his worn T-shirt, then ran a hand through his long brown hair. "I have the feeling that Miss Manners would give all three of us big fat F's."

"I wouldn't go that far. After all, since the

future bride and groom never even showed up for their wedding shower," Kimberly reasoned, "I guess we're off the hook."

"I'll buy that," Josh said, kissing Winnie's spiky hair.

"Me too," Winnie agreed. She reached for the uncut cake and, with one finger, scooped up chocolate icing. Josh did the same.

For a moment all three of them listened to some jocks who were throwing a football up and down the hall. Then they stared at the presents again. Winnie had planned an all-girl surprise wedding shower for Melissa and had invited her old high-school friends Faith Crowley and KC Angeletti, plus new U of S friends Kimberly and Lauren Turnbell-Smythe. At the same time Josh, who lived down the hall, had planned a surprise guy shower for Brooks. But the biggest surprise had been on Winnie and Josh, since Melissa and Brooks had disappeared after Melissa's track meet. The couple hadn't been seen since. No one knew where they had gone.

"Do you think I did something to jinx Mel and Brooks?" Winnie babbled. "What do you think happened to them? I still can't believe Mel didn't come back at all last night. I wish she'd show up. I hope she's okay."

Kimberly cleared a space on Melissa's bed and then climbed onto it. She flipped through one of Melissa's biology books. "If you ask me, I think Mel and Brooks had another fight."

Winnie cringed.

"Sounds likely to me," Josh agreed.

"Then maybe Mel went to her parents' house," Kimberly continued. "You know, she and Brooks are the first freshman couple I've ever known who wanted to get married. They're also the couple I'd nominate as most likely to break up."

"I sure hope that's not what happened," Winnie fretted. "I mean, I know they fight and compete about everything, but that's just the way Melissa is. She's talented and driven. And Brooks is talented and laid-back, so he should balance Melissa and be the perfect guy for her. Right?"

"If you say so," Kimberly said.

Winnie kept babbling. "Maybe it was the whole marriage thing that did it. I mean maybe as soon as you think about making a permanent commitment and you give this *name* to it, you know— marriage—like as soon as you do that, you can only think about breathing on the other

person every morning before they've brushed
their teeth and how they like to eat garlic bagels
before they go to bed and watch every old 'Star
Trek' that was ever made—"

"Whoa, Win," Josh soothed. He crossed his
leg over hers, his torn sweats crisscrossing her
neon tights. "What set you off?"

Winnie shrugged.

"Did we hit a nerve?" Kimberly asked.

"You know me." Winnie tried to laugh. She
fell across Josh's lap. "I'm just one big bundle
of nerves."

They stopped talking as the jocks ran down
the hall again, sounding like a cattle stampede.
Winnie scooped more icing off the cake and
licked her finger pensively.

"You okay, Win?" Josh asked after a moment.
He helped her sit up again. Then he put his
cheek to hers and tapped her single earring,
which was shaped like a refrigerator. "Say something."

For once Winnie couldn't speak. She wasn't
okay, and it wasn't because her surprise wedding
shower had turned out to be a bust. It was the
fear that Kimberly was right. Melissa and Brooks
might have broken up. But it wasn't just the
thought of Melissa and Brooks not making it

that had thrown Winnie into such a state. Melissa was strong. She would survive a breakup. Brooks would survive, too. Faith, Brooks's high-school sweetheart, had dumped him soon after they'd all arrived at U of S, and Brooks had certainly bounced back quickly.

Winnie's panic attack wasn't really about Melissa and Brooks at all. As a psych major, Winnie found herself wondering if any two people could stay together forever. Her own parents hadn't stayed married for very long. She and Josh had already been together almost all freshman year. Sure, they'd had their ups and downs, their breakups and makeups, but now they really were together. And that's what scared her. Winnie loved Josh so much, which made it all the more terrifying to think that they could suddenly break apart again.

As usual, Josh immediately sensed where her head was at. He slipped both his arms around her shoulders.

Winnie looked into his eyes. She touched his cheek and was suddenly embarrassed at the way her feelings had flip-flopped once again. Now she was only thinking about how much she adored him, how when she was close to him, her whole body felt like those volcanoes she used to make in grade school out of baking soda and vinegar.

"What are you thinking, Win?" Josh asked.

Winnie blushed as she noticed Kimberly staring at her, too. "I'm just having my usual crazy, demented thoughts. I mean, can you see a picture of *me* in *Modern Bride?*"

"Sure," Kimberly said, giggling. You'd be wearing the latest purple-and-pink spandex unitard, with its very own Winnie-inspired bride-and-groom glow-in-the-dark earrings that rotate and play the theme to 'The Love Connection.'"

Winnie laughed, feeling carefree again. "I'd set a new outrageous trend. The country—no, the world—wouldn't know what hit them."

"And as the groom, I'd wear a giant computer-nerd pocket protector"

"Yes!" Winnie threw her head back and laughed. "And nothing else!"

Soon they were all laughing, tossing bits of ribbon at each other and decorating the anatomy model that always stood on Melissa's desk.

The laughter didn't stop until Kimberly picked up a bag that had been half-shoved under Winnie's bed. She dug into it and pulled out something green and slick. "Hey, here's a shower present from KC," she said. "It's not even wrapped, but at least KC dropped something off. Did she ever come back to the party last night after I went back to my dorm?"

Winnie shook her head and took the green plastic thing from Kimberly. It was soft and floppy and folded into a square. "KC's been pretty weird lately—and I don't mean her usual Tri Beta sorority weird. I mean sad weird."

"She's is going through a rough time," Josh reminded them.

Winnie unfolded the plastic and realized that it was an inflatable dinosaur. "I know, but look at this. A plastic dinosaur is a pretty strange wedding present, even by my standards."

"At least KC got Melissa something," Josh said. "Win, you and I didn't get a present for them at all yet."

Win began stacking the gifts next to the door. "That's just because wedding presents always seem to be boring kitchen things—toasters, waffle irons, dishes, teapots—like all married people do is cook and eat. I'd rather take more time and get them something truly different and cool."

"Like what?" Kimberly asked.

"Like crampons," Winnie said.

"What-ons?" Kimberly came back.

Josh laughed. "Mr. Mountaineer Brooks has been dying for a pair of those handmade crampons that some guy in Nevada named Joe Tyler invented. They're these things you use for rock climbing. Brooks told me Melissa wanted to learn to climb, too, so we figured it would be a present for both of them."

Winnie nodded. "Josh and I were going to get the crampons sometime before the wedding, but who's got time to drive to Nevada." She walked over to the window and looked out over the huge lawn called "the green." The last few students were leaving breakfast at the dining commons. There was a Frisbee game going on in front of the laundry cave. Winnie realized that she was looking for Melissa or Brooks.

When she didn't see them, her mouth revved up again. "I'm sure it's better if this whole wedding thing is called off, anyway," she rambled. "I've got a monster French test coming up where I have to write an essay—in French—and I've already wasted enough time planning this ultra-successful shower."

"I have a huge research paper due for U.S. history," Josh said.

"That's freshman year for you," Kimberly joked. "Tests. Papers. A few parties. A breakup or two . . ." her voice trailed off as she stared down at the floor.

They were quiet again. Josh began picking up cake crumbs while Kimberly stared down at her old worn-out jazz shoes. Winnie stayed at the window. The longer she looked out onto the green, the more her panic bubbled up again. It was almost as if she were waiting for Melissa and Brooks to walk across it—together—as proof that she and Josh would never split up.

"Maybe the wedding shower didn't happen because of my study guilt," she chattered. "If I'd just studied my French verbs regularly, maybe they would still be engaged. Freshman year would still be perfect and the tooth fairy would live right down the hall!"

Suddenly Winnie jumped as if she'd been snuck up on in a dark alley. She spun around. Her mouth opened and she took another deep breath. It was Josh who'd touched her from behind in an attempt to comfort her.

"I know, I'm out of control," she said. "Shut me up."

Josh kissed her on the mouth, long and hard.

Winnie slid her hands around his waist, not sure if she'd caught her breath or gotten even more charged. Whichever had happened, she felt a little better. She kissed him back.

Kimberly cleared her throat. "Well, I guess I'll leave you two alone." She was almost out the door when she stopped in the doorway and turned back. She leaned against the wall, her tall, lean body looking like a big question mark.

Winnie and Josh let go of one another. "What is it, Kimberly?" Winnie prompted.

Kimberly took a moment. Then she looked at both of them and said, "If Melissa and Brooks did break up, it's probably for the good, you know. If two people can't get along, it's better to figure it out before they promise to stay together forever. Don't you agree with me?"

Winnie and Josh looked at one another.

"Not that two people can't work a lot of things out," Kimberly went on. "But there are some differences that you can never work out." She sighed. "It's like these tragic flaws of the Shakespearian protagonists I studied in fall semester of English lit."

Winnie would have laughed, but she knew

that Kimberly was really talking about Derek Weldon. Derek had been Kimberly's first boyfriend at U of S. For a while they'd been a really tight couple. But they'd recently broken up. Kimberly had sworn that she would never go out with him again.

"Are you thinking about Derek?" Winnie whispered.

Kimberly nodded, then gave an embarrassed smile to Josh, as if discussing one guy in front of another wasn't the proper thing to do. "Derek is great in a lot of ways," she admitted. "He's smart, he shares my interest in science—"

"He's a major hunk," Winnie cracked.

Josh nudged her.

"But he was too jealous," Kimberly added. "And he was jealous for no reason. I won't put up with that. I never want to get involved with him again."

There was a sudden seriousness in the room that took Winnie's breath away.

"I think Derek *was* way too jealous," Josh said after a pause, "but I can relate to how he must have felt." He swallowed. "I'm not the super-jealous type or anything, but Winnie has a tendency to, you know, flirt with other guys. I think that if there was one thing that could break me and Win up—or make me want to break up—it would be if Win really got interested in some other guy." He barely glanced at Winnie. "I couldn't take that."

"What about you, Win?" Kimberly asked. "Is there anything about Josh that could make you want to break up—if you don't mind talking about it."

Winnie wasn't sure if she minded talking about it or not. She just wasn't sure that she *could* talk about it. She was thinking about how she'd always been a boy-crazy flirt who'd gone over the edge for every cute guy who'd said two words to her. She'd cleaned up her act since falling in love with Josh, but old habits died hard. Just thinking that she could slip again and ruin things had given her a lump in her throat.

Josh was staring at her. "Can you answer her, Win?" He laughed nervously. "I know I'm perfect, but there must be a few things that truly drive you crazy and could make you never want to see my face again."

Winnie didn't have to think long to come up with a response. She knew the answer, she just had trouble forming the words. She tried to calm herself by looking at Josh. "I guess it would be if you ever became the living, barely breathing computer lump again," she said, hoping she was being funny. In reality she found nothing humorous about Josh's tendency to tune her out when he got so involved in his work that he practically became one with his computer screen.

Kimberly suddenly clapped her hands, as if she were celebrating some major breakthrough. "Enough confessions," she pronounced. "You two will be together until you're both a hundred and six. You know what your biggest flaws are, and that has to be the first step to dealing with them. Here's to couples being honest."

Winnie turned to Josh. "Right."

He smiled and saluted her. "May we all live happily ever after."

Winnie laughed. "May Brooks and Melissa end up on the 'Newlywed Game.'"

"Uh-oh," Josh cracked, "that sounds like a fate worse than death."

"Wait a minute. Look!" Winnie had turned her head, not even intending to look out the window this time. And that was when she saw Melissa and Brooks, looking lovey-dovier than Winnie had ever seen them. They had their arms around one another and were talking and laughing as they strolled across the green.

"Look!" Winnie shrieked.

"What?" Josh gasped.

Kimberly leaped over to join them. She burst out laughing. "Melissa and Brooks. They sure look together now. That shows how much I know."

Josh nodded. "They look real happy."

"I knew they were okay, I knew it!" Winnie said. She slipped out of Josh's hold and began to run across to the door. Suddenly she felt hopeful and light, as if everything in the world could turn out right. Then she stopped again and stared down at the gifts. She made a terrible, funny face.

"What is it?" Josh prompted.

"The presents," Winnie said, giggling. "We'd better rewrap them all, pronto."

Three

....

A cello sang out across the dining room of the Springfield Country Club. Light sparkled from the chandeliers. The maître d' stepped smartly as he led Faith Crowley across the carpet, past professors, university officers, and local society matrons, who looked up from their dinners and drinks as she walked carefully to her table.

Courtney Conner, the president of KC's sorority was already seated, waiting. She stood up to greet Faith. She wore a black velvet jacket, her Tri Beta pin, and diamond earrings. Her shoulder-length blond hair was held back by a black satin headband.

In comparison, Faith was in her usual cowboy boots and denim, her own blond hair in a straggly braid and her book bag overflowing with playscripts and textbooks. "Hi," she said.

Courtney's smile betrayed none of the distrust that she and Faith had once felt toward one another. In fact, if Faith had wanted to, she could almost believe that this was a purely social get-together, where friendly gossip and chitchat would be exchanged. But it wasn't. It was a meeting of great purpose.

"I'm glad to be here," Faith assured Courtney. "Thanks for calling me and asking me to meet you. This is really a nice place."

Courtney smiled. "Haven't you ever been to the Springfield Country Club before?"

Faith shook her head. "But I will be coming here soon. Two friends of mine are getting married here."

"Oh?" Courtney responded, as if she were waiting to hear more about the upcoming wedding.

Faith realized that she could have gone on about how the groom was actually her own ex-boyfriend, and how Brooks and Melissa had almost eloped, then changed their minds and were now planning a big country-club wedding in less than a week. But she didn't go on about it. She didn't want to get off track and waste time.

"Please sit down," Courtney urged, sitting back down herself. "I like to come here for private talks. It's relaxing. I've already ordered us some food."

Faith wondered how Courtney could find a country club relaxing. To her the place was the definition of uptight: clinking crystal, ostentatious jewelry, subtle intensive stares. She sat down and draped her napkin over her lap.

"I just mean that no one will overhear us," Courtney explained, as if she'd read Faith's mind. "Or rather, no one who matters will overhear us. No one from my sorority, or the dorms, I mean." She smiled. "So we can talk freely."

"Good," Faith said. She took a sip of water.

"Well," Courtney began, pushing the menu aside. "Let's get down to business."

Faith nodded. "We've got to come up with a plan to help KC," she said.

Courtney paused as the waiter gracefully decorated their table with platters of cold cheeses, salads, and meats. She pointed to the food. "I hope this is all right."

Faith smiled and the waiter went on his way.

Courtney scooted her chair in. "Okay. I stopped by the University Health Clinic and got advice from a nurse, although I already knew a lot of what she told me. What about you?"

Faith hesitated. She couldn't quite believe that she was sitting in a country club, chatting so calmly about the drug problem of one of her high-school best friends. *Drug problem. KC!* Faith could barely bring herself to believe it. But believe it or not, the problem was horribly real.

"Winnie introduced me to a substance-abuse counselor who gives advice to the volunteers at the hotline," Faith informed Courtney. "Winnie answers phones there."

Courtney leaned in closer. "And what did the counselor tell you?"

Faith sighed. "That KC really needs her friends right now."

"That's for sure," Courtney agreed.

Faith took a deep breath. "The counselor also said that we may have to do and say things that KC won't like. He said that we may have to step in and stop KC from hurting herself, until she's able to do that on her own." Faith trembled as she remembered the conversation. "The counselor said that it'll be hard on us, but that real friendship takes courage."

Courtney rearranged her silverware with her beautifully manicured hands. "I'm prepared for that. I think I'm one of KC's closest new college friends. I won't let her down."

"I know," Faith said. She smiled. "Neither one of us will."

"But even if KC and I weren't such good friends," Courtney went on, "I would still want to help her. She's also a part of my sorority, and as Tri Beta president it's my responsibility to look out for all pledges and sisters—although my concern for KC goes a lot further than that."

"Of course."

Courtney paused for a moment and seemed to lose her society-girl poise. "The nurse I talked to at the health clinic said some of the same things that the counselor told you. She also talked about how people lose their judgment when they use drugs, how they can really be influenced by other people—usually the wrong people—which is another reason why we both need to step in."

Faith felt guilty for not stepping in weeks before. She'd known something was wrong when KC had missed lectures for the one class they took together—western civ. And when Faith had seen her old friend, beautiful, business major KC looked like she hadn't eaten or slept in weeks. "KC has so much to deal with right now," Faith mumbled, almost to herself. "Her father is so sick. He may be dying."

Courtney looked down.

"And Peter Dvorsky, her boyfriend, went to study in Europe," Faith went on. "I can't believe I've been so busy with classes and plays that I haven't been there for her. It took me so long just to figure out what was wrong."

Courtney shrugged. "You didn't know what to look for."

"But when did I find out," Faith blurted, "I just went on and on about how anyone who takes drugs is a moron." She remembered how KC had tested her, asking what she thought of people who experimented with drugs. Faith had just gone off on an alienating, naive tirade about "just saying no."

Courtney reached across the table and touched Faith's hand. "You can't blame yourself."

"I guess not," Faith stammered, even though she continued to feel guilty and stupid. KC had been asking her for help—begging for help—and Faith hadn't heard her. "I'd just like to make up for the way I let her down before."

Courtney gave her an understanding smile. Then she looked around, as if making sure there really were no sorority spies lurking under the dessert cart. "Don't worry. Hopefully we're still not too late."

"Hopefully not." Faith sipped her water. "But what can we do?"

"I'm not completely sure," Courtney said, as she arranged a plate of cold cuts for Faith and then one for herself. "That's why I wanted to talk to you. I think we need to work together. The only thing I know for sure is who we're up against."

"What do you mean?" Faith asked, picking at her food.

"I mean, KC hasn't gotten into this all by herself," Courtney said. "Unfortunately she's had help."

"From who?"

"Marielle Danner."

"Marielle?" Faith barely knew Marielle. All she remembered was that Marielle was a spoiled sophomore who had been kicked out of the Tri Betas, and now lived next door to KC in

Langston House, KC's all-girl, all-single-room dorm. "What does Marielle have to do with this?"

"Lots." Courtney put down her fork. "I've had some of my Tri Beta sisters do a little asking around—and a little spying," she confessed. "Marielle began using drugs after she left my sorority. She's been hanging out with some truly worthless types, and she's worked very hard to bring KC into her crowd."

"Great," Faith groaned.

"I know." Courtney nodded, her refined voice rising in anger. "Marielle has supplied KC with all kinds of pills. From what I can tell, KC takes ups until she's about to crack, then gets downs from Marielle just so she can go to sleep. She's probably so wiped out the next day that she does the same thing all over again just to get herself to class."

Faith was a little shocked to hear Courtney talk about all this so bluntly.

Courtney didn't pause. "As far as I know, Marielle buys the drugs and has been giving or selling them to KC. At least KC isn't making buys and she certainly isn't dealing, or anything like that—as far as I know."

Faith just stared at her. "I guess you talked to

the health-clinic nurse for a long time."

"No. Not long." Courtney finally gave an embarrassed smile. "I already knew a lot about this. My older brother had a drug problem. I've seen this whole thing before. And I know how terrible it can get. That's why we have to step in now, before KC really messes up her life."

Faith was suddenly on the verge of tears. When she'd first met Courtney, she and Winnie had assumed that the Tri Beta president was some brittle sorority snob. She was beginning to realize that KC couldn't have made a better choice of a new close friend. "I just wish I'd listened when KC tried to talk to me before!"

"Don't torture yourself," Courtney said. "You still have lots of time. Let me tell you my plan, and then you tell me if you want in."

"Okay." Faith pressed her napkin to her face.

Courtney took a deep breath. "This may sound shallow," she began, "but my position as president of the Tri Beta is too visible for me to be connected with a drug user. I can't risk harming the reputaion of my house and those in it."

Faith nodded, listening carefully.

"That's why I need your help," Courtney

explained. "What I have in mind is a two-part plan to help KC. I think we can both agree that Marielle Danner has to be kept away from her. It's like what the nurse at the health clinic said; KC's judgment is impaired. She's getting dependent on Marielle. Marielle can control her. As long as that continues, KC hasn't got a chance."

"I agree, but how do we make Marielle leave KC alone?"

"Well I'm not sure about that yet," Courtney admitted. "I am sure, though, that there's got to be some way to get the message across."

She leaned over the table. "That leaves you the even more difficult task of watching and somehow protecting KC. I'm not sure what you'll need to do, Faith. If you try and talk to her right now, she probably won't listen to you. I just think you should look out for her, find out what she's up to, and if she needs you, then just be there for her."

A sob was pressing at Faith's throat again. "I can do that," she promised. "I didn't do it before, but I won't let anything stop me from doing it now."

"Thanks." Courtney smiled, her face less anxious, her demeanor more relaxed. She raised her water goblet. "Here's to our friend," she said quietly.

Faith raised her own glass, too. "Yes. Here's to KC."

"Oh God, is that really the curb?"

"Yes, KC."

"It looks like it's about a fifteen-foot drop."

Only a few blocks away from the Springfield Country Club, KC swayed and stumbled. Her eyes were so bleary she could barely make out the concrete under her feet. She had never felt quite so woozy before. The music that had been playing inside the Blue Parrot, the downtown dance hangout she and Marielle Danner had just left, still throbbed in her ears. And the little yellow pills Marielle had given her weren't helping.

"You are so goony, KC," Marielle chanted. "You are queen of the goon birds."

For some reason Marielle thought that remark was the funniest thing that had ever been said. She began to giggle and choke and pant, ending up down on her knees on the sidewalk. She'd always been slim, but she was starting to look emaciated. Her dark hair was tangled and her once-perfect skin looked blotchy. Even her red blazer, an expensive holdover from her Tri Beta days, was wrinkled and stained.

"Marielle," KC moaned.

"What?"

"Can you stand up?"

"No," Marielle sputtered, "I'm laughing too hard."

"Well, my head feels terrible."

Marielle giggled. "That's because you need another up. You're starting to come down. You don't want to do that yet." She clawed at her expensive shoulder bag and produced the clear plastic bag that had held this evening's ration of pills. "Ah-oh," Marielle cautioned, "we're running on empty." She giggled again.

It was no laughing matter for KC. She really *did* feel horrible. She wanted to take anything to feel better right now—*anything* to wipe out the thoughts that crept back whenever she started to come down: thoughts of Peter being so far away, and how their conversations were getting more forced and weird each time they talked; thoughts of the term papers she hadn't started and the class assignments she hadn't read; and worst of all, thoughts of her father and how the last time she'd seen him he barely had the energy to talk to her. The little hair he had left had turned white. He'd lost almost thirty pounds and the chemotherapy had given his skin an iridescent glow.

But while KC's head was flooded with painful reminders, Marielle just giggled and hummed.

"Look," KC finally said, "I'm going back to the dorm. I really don't feel well."

"You're not going anywhere," Marielle insisted. She grabbed KC's arm. "The fun has just started. That was only our first club and the night is still young. Let's go find the rest of the gang. It's not even *midnight*."

KC sighed and thought how only a few short weeks ago midnight was the deadline she gave herself to get all her studying done. With Marielle it was just the starting point of an evening. KC felt a pang of nostalgia for the old days when her life was so disciplined and controlled. She suddenly missed Courtney and the rest of her sorority. And she missed her old security blankets—Winnie and Faith. But lately her blankets hadn't been around, and in their place were Marielle's pills. The problem was the pills got used up, and when they were gone, KC was left feeling terrible and empty.

Marielle had finally stopped laughing and

seemed to be reading KC's mind. "What's wrong, pal?" she queried. "Got the no-bennies blues?"

KC shrugged. She watched blankly as a car splashed through a pothole on the dimly lit street.

"I feel the same way. What we have to arrange for," Marielle continued confidently, "is a sale."

"A what?"

"A sale. A buy. A purchase, you innocent little sorority freak." Marielle started laughing again, and soon she was giggling out of control. "You know, I can't supply you forever, you little baby. You have to learn to take care of yourself, KC. You know, good old self-reliance. You need to grow up."

KC wasn't sure she knew what Marielle meant. Her head hurt. Her stomach felt funny. Things looked blurry. She had an ashy taste in her mouth. "What are you talking about?"

Marielle clapped an arm around KC's shoulder and began to steer her across the street. "Well, we're not going to do it right now, dingbat head. But next time I'll set it up for you. I'll show you how it's done, and you'll pick up the stuff. You'll make the buy—if you know what I mean."

KC wasn't at all sure what she meant.

Marielle didn't seem to care. "You'll find out," she howled. "I'll arrange the whole thing. You'll do great. It's time for you to go shopping without Mom and become a very big girl."

KC didn't try to understand. She simply followed Marielle down the dark, downtown street.

Four

....

"Winnie, I thought you didn't like to eat hotcakes," said Lauren Turnbell-Smythe as she watched Winnie stuff her mouth.

"Yeah, in fact I thought you didn't like to eat breakfast, period," Melissa exclaimed.

Winnie made a face. "People always think stuff about me that's not true. I *love* hotcakes. I love everything right now. I'm in a fabulous mood." She laughed and put a reassuring arm around Melissa. "Aren't you in a good mood, too?"

Melissa looked at her friends. Winnie wasn't

the only one grinning at her. Faith, Kimberly, and Lauren were also stuffing their mouths with dining-commons pancakes and celebrating. The breakfast was supposed to make up for the wedding shower that Melissa hadn't known about. Brooks was at the next table with Josh and Kimberly's ex, Derek Weldon.

Melissa *was* in a good mood. Since deciding to have a big wedding, she'd felt as if she could sail in the air like a helium balloon. But she was so unused to feeling this way that she wasn't ready to admit it. "I can see you're feeling good," she told Winnie.

"I'm probably just having some unstable mood swing," Winnie cracked. She flicked some orange juice at Faith. "I learned all about that in Psych 101."

Faith laughed.

"Things can't be too perfect, Melissa. You still have to put up with us," Kimberly said, giggling. She touched Melissa's hand, then cast a short, uncomfortable glance at Derek, who was glaring at her from the next table. As soon as he saw Kimberly looking at him, he turned away. "But it could be worse."

Melissa shrugged, the most optimistic gesture she was ready to share. Then she met Brooks's eyes. He was obviously taking some teasing from Josh and Derek, but he leaned away from his table to smile at her. In spite of herself she shared that smile with Winnie, Faith, Kimberly, and Lauren.

The four girls all grinned, too. And blushed. For a moment no one said anything. No one needed to.

"It's just all a little unbelievable," Melissa confessed, feeling the heat on her freckled cheeks.

"It's all pretty rushed," Kimberly came back.

"*I* feel rushed," Lauren spoke up. "And the only thing I have to arrange is giving up my rented room and taking Melissa's place in the dorms." She looked at Melissa. "I can't believe you're actually getting married."

Winnie tipped her head toward Lauren's shoulder. "That's okay, Lauren. Moving in with me may be more traumatic than getting married."

Faith laughed again. "It does seem like it's all happening pretty fast now," she said to Melissa. "The wedding rehearsal is Saturday night and the wedding this Sunday."

Melissa tried to calm the excitement she felt inside. Everything was moving unbelievably fast.

It was as if Brooks's relatives had been waiting for the word "go!" and they were off, running the wedding race. "This Sunday was the only time the Springfield Country Club was available," Melissa told them. "Unless we wanted to wait another four months. And it turned out that this weekend was a good time for Brooks's family, so we just decided to go with it."

"To go with it!" Winnie repeated. "Is that really Melissa McDormand I hear?"

Now it was Melissa's turn to laugh. She couldn't help it. She no longer felt as if she was tottering at the edge of a cliff, about to plummet at any second. Instead she was starting to feel as if she could throw herself off a cliff and sail in the breeze.

"Do you like Brooks's family?" Faith asked. "They can be a little overwhelming."

"No, they're all great," Melissa said. "Brooks just seems to have so many relatives."

Again, the girls were quiet, as if Melissa's delight were more than any of them could quite handle. Melissa looked from face to face. Kimberly was so hip and witty. Faith so comforting—even if she was Brooks's ex. Winnie was so funny and Lauren so sweet. The four girls felt like Melissa's family now, especially since she'd asked them to be her bridesmaids.

"We all have to meet on Wednesday at the bridal shop for fittings. Don't anyone miss it," Melissa reminded them. "They've told us about ten times how little time they have to do alterations."

"I'll be there," Kimberly said.

Lauren nodded.

"Me too," said Faith.

"Hey, talk about alterations," Winnie announced. "I'm all for this alteration in you, Mel." She suddenly grew serious. "I'm really happy for you. You deserve it."

"I agree," whispered Lauren.

"Hear, hear," chirped Kimberly.

Faith put her hand on Melissa's arm. "I wish you and Brooks all the best."

Melissa felt the sting of joyful tears. She looked back at Brooks, but this time she didn't catch his eye. He had a faraway look, as if Josh and Derek were talking so fast that he couldn't quite follow. But even that slightly hazy look on his face just made her love him more. No more being scared. No more running. Just pure generous love.

Melissa turned to her four girlfriends again

and was still flooded with that frothy feeling. "You know, sometimes it's hard for me to admit when things are good," she suddenly told them in a loud, clear voice.

Faith, Kimberly, and Lauren looked stunned. Winnie was actually quiet.

"I just want to say that I'm so happy that Brooks and I are getting married. And I'm happy that I have the four of you as my friends."

"I'm telling you it's going to be the end of your life, Brooks," Derek said at the next table. He pushed up his wire-rim glasses, shifted in his preppy polo shirt, then glanced briefly at Kimberly. "Marriage is like being in jail. Promising your life to some girl? What a frightening thought."

Josh laughed. "Depends on the girl." He gave Brooks a supportive pat. "But I have to admit that the old M word is pretty scary. Come on, Baldwin, tell us the truth. Under that cool, honors'-college, mountain-climber exterior, you're really shaking like a leaf."

"Not me," Brooks said, smiling. "I'm ready. And willing."

Derek shook his head.

Josh laughed.

Brooks wasn't fazed. As far as he could tell, he wasn't scared at all. If anything, he felt braver, stronger, and more secure than ever before. He snuck a look at Melissa, managing to meet her eyes for a quick, shared grin. "Sorry, guys," he said, beaming and shoveling pancakes into his mouth. "I'd like to be able to say that I'm as much of a wimp as you two, but it's just not true."

Derek sat up taller. "It's not a question of wimpishness," he argued, glancing at Kimberly. "It's a question of good sense. Trusting your life to some female," he said with a hint of bitterness, "is like throwing yourself into battle without your armor on."

Josh and Brooks exchanged smiles.

"Gee, Derek. Your attitude couldn't have anything to do with the fact that Kimberly gave you the old dumpola," Josh hinted.

Derek stared down at his plate. "No way," he said with mock coolness. "This has nothing to do with me. Brooks is the one looking at thirty years to life."

"That's okay with me," said Brooks. "It'll be a life sentence in paradise." He thought about

Derek's image of a warrior in armor.
Sometimes that's how Melissa made him feel
when she was arguing and fighting with him.
But even at her most contrary, Melissa needed
him. She was from a troubled family, and even
though she was incredibly smart and talented,
she was also incredibly insecure. She needed to
be taken care of. Brooks loved the idea of being
the knight on the horse who sweeps in to save
the day.

"Don't listen to Derek," Josh counseled.
"You and Mel will be great together."

Derek grunted.

"Say whatever you want, Derek," Brooks said,
still thinking about Melissa and how much she
needed him. "It's not going to sway me."

The three guys dug into their food while the
girls huddled over their table and giggled.

Josh gestured to Winnie. "I can imagine
loving some girl for the rest of my life," he
said. "It's just making the decision to get
married that seems so weird. I think if I was
going to get hitched, I'd have to not think
about it. It'd have to be kind of like your first
swimming lesson. Just close your eyes and
jump."

"You mean, close your eyes and drown,"

Derek groaned. He pushed his food tray away. "And there's something else to think about. Brooks, do you realize that you are promising never to ask out, drool over, lust over, or write secret love notes to any other female, ever again?"

"I think Brooks knows that." Josh smirked. "But you know, Derek, it's kind of amazing that you're bringing it up, considering that you went atomic at the idea of Kimberly just talking to another guy."

Derek folded his arms, and didn't say another word.

Josh gave Brooks a sympathetic look. "I really don't think jealousy is a great basis for a lasting relationship," he said.

Brooks shrugged. "It's okay. The only girl I want to drool over is Melissa."

Josh looked over at red-haired Melissa, who was leaning into Faith and laughing. "I don't blame you, even though Melissa isn't exactly my type." He tugged on his earring. "Personally I go for the slightly demented types who borrow my boxer shorts so they can wear them to important social occasions."

"Anyone I know?" a female voice suddenly intruded.

All three guys looked up to see Winnie suddenly hovering over their table. She grabbed Josh's juice glass out of his hand, took a sip, then handed it back before Josh had put his hand down.

Winnie kissed Josh's ear. "I don't want to intrude on any male bonding going on here, but I came to say good-bye. "My French test is next period." She rolled her eyes. "I have to write an essay in French on Madame Tortura— better known as Madame the Torturer's—topic of choice." She pulled a French/English dictionary out of her book bag. "At least we get some help. This dictionary is the only thing that will save me."

"Good luck," Josh told her.

"Thanks. And good luck to you," Winnie said to Brooks. She brightened. "Oh Brooks, Lauren and I were talking about throwing another party for you and Melissa on Friday night. The big-wedding eve. Melissa plans to show this time. I thought we could just have a blowout in our dorm room. Okay with you?"

"Count me in," Brooks said, smiling.

"Great. There's just one more thing. I say we have to take advantage of your last few days of bachelorhood by doing rites-of-passage stuff.

It's very important—I read about it in my psych book."

Josh laughed.

Winnie put her dictionary down next to him, then sidled over to Brooks. "I'll start the first ritual right now. "She leaned over and planted a quick kiss on Brooks's cheek. Then she stood up and shouted to the entire dining hall. *"All girls have to kiss this dude before leaving breakfast!"*

Heads turned. Brooks blushed.

"Last chance!" Winnie yelled, already on her way out. *"He's getting married on Sunday."* She blew one last kiss to Josh, then raced out the door.

Derek watched her, then looked at Josh. "I may be overly jealous, but I wouldn't want my girlfriend kissing other guys."

Josh laughed. "Lighten up, Derek. Just because you ruined things with Kimberly doesn't mean I have to do the same thing with Winnie." He looked down and noticed Winnie's dictionary sitting next to his tray. He grabbed it. "Great, she forgot her dictionary," he mumbled. "I better get this to her before she freaks out."

"That's all women ever do," Derek said, "freak out about every little thing."

"Man, that's so upbeat and accurate," Josh answered as he slung on his leather jacket. "Remind me to consult you when hell freezes over." He patted Brooks on the shoulder, then ran out.

Derek shook his head. "Running after girls." He sighed. "You'll never catch me doing that again."

Brooks, too, was getting tired of Derek's bitterness. But before he could stand up to go, Kimberly, Lauren, and Faith walked over.

"Maybe the whole dining commons doesn't have to kiss you, but I will," Kimberly said. She ignored Derek's glare and planted a kiss on the top of Brooks's head. "Congrats. I really think it's great that you and Melissa worked everything out. I wish you the best."

"Me too," Lauren added in a shy whisper. She leaned in, kissed her finger, then planted the kiss on Brooks's arm.

"Thanks," Brooks said.

Kimberly and Lauren backed away to clear their trays.

Before Brooks realized it, Faith was right next to him. Her hair was in a French braid and she was wearing a pair of faded overalls he remembered from their high-school days when they had been a tight couple.

"Hi," Faith said simply. "I thought I'd give you a good-luck kiss, too."

She lightly touched his shoulder, then leaned down to kiss his cheek. Without meaning to, Brooks turned his head so that his lips just barely brushed Faith's as she moved toward him. The kiss was light and quick, but it lingered on his mouth as if she'd burned him.

Faith pulled back, pretending that nothing odd had happened.

Brooks, on the other hand, stared down at the table. Suddenly the image he'd had of himself as some knight atop a white horse faded away. Instead he was full of the familiar scent of Faith's skin, the feel of her long hair. He was back in high school, at dances, taking long walks home through grassy fields, necking in his father's car. His heart raced.

But Faith was already clutching her book bag and moving away.

"I have to go to class," she called. "I'll see you Friday night at the party. And of course I'll see you at the wedding and the rehearsal. I wouldn't miss that for anything."

Brooks just nodded and pushed back his chair.

"See you," Faith called for the last time. Kimberly and Lauren joined her, then all three girls walked out onto the green.

"See you," Derek grumped as he stared after Kimberly again.

Brooks ignored Derek. Instead he made himself focus on Melissa, who had cleared away her tray and was talking to a track teammate. He stared at her strong, athletic body and the way the light glistened off her red hair. She was beautiful and special. She was his princess and he loved her more than anyone.

Five

•••••••••••••••••••

reat day, huh?"

"Beautiful," Kimberly said. She looked up at the sky.

It was a crisp spring day, sunny but cool, smelling of cut grass and wind, a day that was asking to be enjoyed, but as Kimberly walked back across the dorm green with Lauren, she knew she was stuck in a bad mood.

The reason was Derek.

She had tried to ignore him, but his presence at breakfast had been enough to give her indigestion. "Do you have writing class right now?" she asked Lauren.

"Not right away. I'm free for the next hour."

"Me too." Kimberly kicked some water that had collected outside the laundry cave. "My first class isn't until eleven."

Lauren gave her a tentative smile.

They kept walking, heading aimlessly toward the new, sterile-looking dorms that were often referred to as "the motels." The sun kept shining, the dew on the grass shone, but Kimberly just kept thinking about Derek. He'd been like some black cloud all through breakfast. His glares had seemed to say, "The reason we're no longer together is your fault, Kimberly Dayton! You are a heartless girl, while I am just an innocent freshman guy." Yeah, right. How innocent was it to go crazy with jealousy over something that never even happened?

"Are you okay?" Lauren suddenly asked.

"Me?"

Lauren stopped walking. "Yes, you. I don't want to pry or anything, but you seem kind of upset about something."

"I'm fine," Kimberly decided. "I'm just sick of Derek, and I hope breakfast is the last time I have to be near him."

"Except for Melissa's wedding," Lauren reminded her.

Kimberly shrugged. "Except for that." They

began walking again. "It's stupid for me to stew about him. After all, *I* broke up with *him*. I'm totally sure I did the right thing. And I really am not interested in speaking to him ever again." She slapped her hands together, as if getting rid of crumbs. "So that's that."

Lauren sighed.

"What about you?" Kimberly asked. "I haven't really talked to you since that whole thing happened with Dimitri. Are *you* all right?"

Lauren didn't change her pace or even her expression, and yet Kimberly felt that everything about her was different. Dimitri Costigan Broder was a smooth-talking athlete who'd stolen Lauren's heart, only to turn out to be a liar and a fake. Lauren had fallen so hard for him that he had made her forget her first love, Dash Ramirez. But now both guys were history, and Lauren looked sad and lost. She clung to her expensive leather bag and looked up at the blue sky.

"Do you want to talk about it?" Kimberly prompted.

Lauren shrugged.

"It's okay," Kimberly soothed. "I know how things can get sometimes. I think guys were put on this planet to give women nothing but one-hundred-and-ten-percent grief."

Lauren sat down on a bench and folded her pale hands in her lap. "I do want to talk about it," she said. "I *need* to talk about it." She took a deep breath. "Ever since I've been living alone off campus, I've been feeling more and more cut off. I don't talk to people enough, I guess."

Kimberly sat down next to her. "Have you heard from Dimitri?"

Lauren shook her head. "Not a word," she answered softly. "And I don't think I'll ever try to get in touch with him. Still, I've been thinking about a lot of things since the police took him away."

Dimitri had been arrested after his last track meet. He'd been charged with fraud for lying to the university about his background.

"I hurt and things are rough. . . ." Lauren's voice trailed off, but her delicate face took on a determined look. "But you know what?"

"What?" Kimberly whispered.

Lauren looked up, her skin looking like white velvet, even under the bright sun. "I'm not sorry it happened. I'm not sorry I met him or felt so strongly about him, even though it turned out so badly." She smiled. "Now I'm just eager to get on with my life."

Kimberly put her arm around Lauren and gave her a hug. "Sounds like a good idea to me." She sat straight again. "You know, that's how I felt after I realized that I didn't want to be a dance major after all. It was really hard to find a new focus. I needed to accept that something new was beginning, instead of something just coming to an end. Now I couldn't be happier being a science major."

Lauren laughed slightly.

"What about Dash?" Kimberly couldn't help asking.

Lauren's face darkened again. "I don't know," she said, sighing. "I can't really think about him yet. There's something between us, or at least *I* feel like there still is. But we'll just have to wait and see. Right now all I can think about are my classes."

Kimberly didn't want to push the issue. Even she knew that newspaper editor Dash Ramirez was Lauren's first, great love. She changed the subject. "And getting our dresses for Mel's wedding."

Lauren nodded. "And that."

Kimberly nudged her. "Hey, what about your

move! When are you officially taking Melissa's place in Forest Hall?"

Lauren's face lit up. Her violet eyes took on a new brightness and for the first time she really smiled. "That's the one thing that's really cheering me up," she said quickly. "I'm so sick of living alone, and living off campus, I can't tell you. I already bought Melissa's dorm contract so I can take her place and room with Winnie."

"Well, one thing about living with Winnie," Kimberly joked. "You'll never have to worry about not having somebody to talk to."

Lauren started to laugh. "That's right. I'll just have to figure out a way to get Winnie to shut up."

"Tell me about it!" Kimberly stood up, then offered a hand and pulled Lauren to her feet. "No, really," she said with more seriousness. "I think you and Winnie will be a great combo."

"I think so, too." Looking a lot cheerier, Lauren pointed toward Forest Hall. Some jocks were pouring out the front door, tossing a basketball back and forth, then dribbling it down the steps. At the same time someone was threatening to empty a beer can on them from the floor above.

Kimberly and Lauren paused to watch.

"Welcome back to the dorms," Kimberly said with a wink.

Lauren smiled. "Actually I thought I'd stop by Forest Hall right now and make sure I could store my things in the basement if I move stuff over early."

"Why don't I help you pack and move some things?" Kimberly offered. "You don't have to do it alone."

Lauren looked delighted. "Would you do that?"

"No. I was just offering so I could back out at the last minute," Kimberly joked. "Of course I'd do it. What are friends for?"

"Thanks."

Kimberly shrugged. "We could do it Thursday morning. We're meeting Melissa down at the bridal shop on Wednesday, right?"

"That's right."

"So I'll come over Thursday morning," Kimberly confirmed. "See you then."

Lauren waved, then went slowly into Forest Hall, dodging the jocks who didn't stop their game to let her pass. Kimberly turned around and headed across the green again, to Coleridge Hall, her dorm, which was in a complex of brick buildings built in the fifties. Coleridge was the creative-arts dorm. Even though Kimberly was no longer a dance major, she still lived there, next door to Faith and Faith's roommate, Liza Ruff.

Kimberly jogged into the Coleridge lobby, past some musicians getting together for a jam session. She checked the bulletin board, which was cramped with performance notices and ride shares, and then trotted up the stairwell. When she got to the second floor, she passed an art major painting a mural on the dorm wall, then paused to find her key. She was glad she'd gone out of her way to cheer up Lauren. She no longer felt angry at Derek, or grumpy or frustrated.

Unfortunately her newfound good mood didn't last very long.

"What?" she blurted.

A bouquet of flowers was resting in front of her door. Actually the bouquet was so huge that she wondered why she hadn't smelled it immediately, then figured it was only because of the fumes of the artist's oil paint down the hall.

"No, please, no," she muttered.

Still praying that the flowers weren't from who she thought they were from, Kimberly reached down and plucked the envelope that had been taped to the wrapping. She read it quickly.

> *Kimberly:*
> *You are the most beautiful, amazing, and intelligent woman on campus. I know that you are determined to ignore me, but you will change your mind. I will make you change your mind. I'm not giving up.*

"*Yuck!*" Kimberly screamed. She quickly stuffed the card back into the envelope. How could Derek act like such a heel that at breakfast, then bombard her with a love note and flowers? What a royal creep! It was worse than creepy, she decided. It was pathetic. Hoping that no one else would see the flowers, she scooped them up and put the key in her lock. But just then, as if on cue, a voice that Kimberly didn't want to hear, rattled down the hallway.

"*Kimberleeeeee!*"

Kimberly whirled around. It was Liza Ruff, bulging out of a leopard-print halter top, which was barely covered up by a bright green sweater. Liza's brassy red hair was a mass of curls, and even the shade of her lipstick made Kimberly want to put sunglasses on. Liza was as unlike Faith as a peacock was unlike a bunny rabbit.

"What is it?" Kimberly asked.

"Ooooo. Touchy. Touchy," Liza sang in response. She grabbed the flowers out of Kimberly's hand, showing off fingernails painted green, yellow, pink, and black. "And what's this? Flowers? No. Not just flowers, an entire floral display. For me?"

Kimberly didn't bother to correct her.

Liza plucked the envelope and card from Kimberly, too, then quickly covered up her disappointment when she saw that the flowers weren't for her after all. "Well, la-di-da," she whined. "This boy has got it bad for you, Kimberly."

"Lucky me," Kimberly tossed back.

Liza pouted. "Well, I know I don't get bouquets this big from admirers unless they're pretty darned serious. I'd take advantage of it if I were you."

Kimberly felt herself bubbling over with frustration. First Derek had spoiled breakfast for her, and now Liza was being a busybody royal pain.

Suddenly she had an idea. She backed away from Liza and pointed at the bouquet. "Look, if you like the flowers so much, why don't you take them." "And him, too," she wanted to add.

"Really?" Liza gasped.

"Really," Kimberly echoed.

Liza staggered backward. Kimberly guessed that she was already making up stories about the fabulous admirer or Hollywood producer who had sent them to her. "Gee, okay. I mean, if you say so. Sure, I'll take them. Wow."

"Enjoy them," Kimberly said as she slammed her way into her room. When she got inside, she groaned and threw herself down on her bed. It wasn't supposed to work this way, she told herself. Flowers were supposed to make you feel good.

But it didn't work that way when they came from the wrong guy.

Six
....

"*I* s it *coudre* or *courir* or *couter*?"

Winnie winced. She couldn't remember. She was still out of breath after leaving the dining commons and racing across campus. She'd stopped at the student union for a chocolate bar to give her a midexam sugar rush, then realized that she'd left her wallet on the counter. By the time she'd run back to fetch it—and luckily it had still been there—and raced back to Kremer Hall, she was ten minutes away from the beginning of her big French exam and couldn't remember either the spelling or the exact definition of one of the hundreds of verbs she might use in her essay.

I'll just check my dictionary, she told herself.

She sat down on the hall bench. The previous class was still in Madame Tortura's room, finishing up their essays. Between the closed door and the dead quiet, she was starting to get the creeps. Her classmates were collecting on the hall floor, poring over last-minute crib sheets. Winnie figured that she should join the crowd. She had to dive into her book bag and pull out her battered English/French, French/English dictionary.

But as she shoveled paper after paper, candy wrapper after candy wrapper out of her bag, a surge of terror went through her. "It's not here," she whispered, her hands whirring through the bag like the front paws of a terrier. "Oh God. I had it at breakfast. Where is it!"

She didn't mean to say it that loudly. Winnie never meant to say *anything* that loudly. When she looked up, she noticed that in spite of the last-minute study pressure, her classmates were staring at her.

"Um, sorry," Winnie said self-consciously. She noticed the girl who sat next to her, Marion Gerstein, and gave her a big smile. "I think I may need some help," Winnie hinted.

"Oh really?" Marion said snidely. "Well, don't look at me. I plan to concentrate on this test."

Winnie didn't bother to explain that all she wanted was to share Marion's dictionary.

Well, pooh pooh on you, Winnie thought. She didn't need help from someone who'd do anything to protect their own grade on the curve. Even if Marion's *dictionnaire* came served on a platter with a croissant next to it, she'd rather flunk the test.

But, on the other hand, *passing* the test was the whole point.

Winnie looked around. Who else would be more cooperative, less selfish, and willing to pitch a dictionary over to her fast, fast, fast? As she watched her classmates, all heads down deep into their vocabulary sheets, she knew that she'd blown it once again. And Marion or no Marion, it was no one's fault but her own. She was doomed.

Just as Winnie was thinking about asking for an incomplete, Madame Tortura's door opened, and her previous class began to drag out one by one. They all looked like they'd barely survived some horrible interrogation. Winnie figured that she would soon feel that same way—even without taking the test, until she saw a familiar face walk out with the rest of the French students. He wore a black turtleneck, karate pants, and Chinese shoes, and he still cut his hair with a little rattail squiggling down his neck.

Winnie leaped to her feet. *"Matthew!"* she cried.

Matthew Callender stopped and looked around. Winnie had dated him when she'd first arrived at U of S. He was into anything and everything weird and ridiculous about American culture, from beauty pageants to hot-dog stands. She'd dumped him soon after their first date and wondered if he still held that against her.

"Winnie," he answered in a cool voice. "What a pleasant surprise."

He still held it against her, Winnie knew instantly. Nonetheless she walked right up to him. "I didn't know you took Madame the Torturer's nine o'clock," she said with forced enthusiasm.

"I don't," he answered, still icy. "I'm in her three o'clock. But she let me take the test early because I have a business appointment this afternoon."

Winnie looked impressed. Matthew had produced a successful U of S calendar, with KC as one of the star models. "Ever the entrepreneur. That's great."

Matthew smiled, very full of himself. "I'm thinking of doing another calendar," he mentioned. "Have you seen KC? I haven't talked to her lately."

Thinking about KC almost cut through Winnie's exam panic. She knew that something was terribly wrong with her old friend, but she wasn't sure what to do about it. "KC's still around," she answered. "Getting involved in a project would probably do her a lot of good right now." She looked at the hall clock. Five minutes to her exam. It was time to get to the point. "Listen, Matthew. I forgot my dictionary for the French essay test. Um, do you think maybe I could borrow yours?"

Matthew stepped back and rolled his eyes. Winnie knew she was done for. "Oh, this is classic." He sighed. "Just classic."

"What?" Winnie managed, even though she knew exactly what he meant.

"Don't play dumb, Winnie," Matthew shot back. "It always amazes me how people who once had no use for you suddenly change their tune when they need something."

"You bozo," Winnie wanted to scream as she

followed him. She wished she could dump him all over again for being such a pompous, self-important dweeb. But she needed his dictionary. So she decided on the only tactic she thought might work. She leaped in front of him, put her hand on his arm, and batted her eyes.

"Matthew," she flirted, "how can you say that? I've barely seen you since last fall."

He stared at her.

"And I've missed you," she lied. She toyed with his corny beaded bracelet. "It's really great to run into you again."

He started to soften. "Really?"

She grinned and moved closer. "Oh yes. Really. You look great, Matthew. I've actually been thinking about you lately." She wondered if he believed her. If he did, maybe a switch in majors was in order. Acting might really be her calling.

"You have?"

Winnie stared at his dictionary. "You are one of the most interesting offbeat characters I know, Matthew. And we weird offbeat types have to stick together." She grinned and tugged his shirt. "That means helping each other out, don't you think?"

Matthew was smiling at her with that cocky

grin of his. He tugged her belt, then nudged her with his hip. When he obviously felt that she was truly pining over him, he plucked his dictionary from under his arm. He was just handing it to her when Winnie heard another familiar voice rise above the din in the hall.

"Gottlieb, you left your dictionary in the dining commons."

It was Josh. But instead of bouncing down the hall to deliver her dictionary like a giant Easter Bunny, he was frozen in place—more like Bambi in a hunter's headlights. Winnie instantly knew why. He'd caught her flirting— the one thing that he said could break them up.

Matthew looked first at Winnie, then at Josh, then at Winnie again. He backed away. "Guess you don't need me now—or anytime in the future." He sneered. Snatching his dictionary out of Winnie's hand, he joined the flow of students heading out of Kremer Hall.

Josh stood his ground. He handed Winnie's dictionary over right away, but his green eyes were still cold.

Winnie's panic found its usual outlet—her mouth. "Josh, I can explain everything," she blurted. "It's not what you think. I was just trying to borrow Matthew's dictionary. I know it was kind of slimy and manipulative of me to flirt with him, but I was desperate. I've worked hard in French all year. I didn't want to flunk this test, and the people in my class are too selfish to help me out."

Despite her explanation Winnie was prepared to see Josh turn and run down the hallway, in that patented Josh I'm-outta-here way of dealing with her flakiness. And who could blame him? Winnie probably presented more problems to the average boyfriend then being in love with a she-gorilla.

But Josh didn't take off. A mix of emotions swept over his face. She couldn't read them all. She could only hope.

"Um . . ." Josh said.

Winnie looked at him pleadingly.

"Um. Let's forget this," Josh said. "It's cool."

"It's what?" Winnie breathed.

"Cool," Josh said. "I understand. I mean, if I were Matthew, I'd probably put out a contract on your life. But since I'm not, let's not worry about it. Go take your test. Get an A. I'll see you back at the dorms."

Winnie couldn't believe it. "Does that mean

like the two of us are still, um . . . cool?"

"Yeah." He laughed. "I know you're telling the truth, Win. Even you couldn't go for a fool like that."

Winnie threw her arms around Josh's neck. He threw his around hers. They hugged as tight as polar bears. Then the bell rang, and Winnie ran into her class to write her essay.

Down in the basement room of the Tri Beta sorority, the mood was as quiet and intense as if an important exam were going on. Courtney had called a special meeting. She pulled the drapes, then sat down at the head of the table.

"Thanks for coming," she said. "I know you all have studying to do."

"That's okay," answered Diane Woo, the Tri Beta secretary. She got up one last time to make sure that the door was securely closed. Then she sat down again and folded her hands. "We all know how important this is."

"Good." Courtney looked around the table at five more of her most trusted sorority sisters. The rest of the Tri Betas were either in class or had been intentionally left out. Courtney only wanted help from girls who would truly help—

girls who would keep their mouths shut. "Has anyone seen or talked to KC since I talked to all of you?"

Glances were exchanged around the table. Diane shook her head.

"I stopped by her dorm the other day, but she wasn't there," said Regina Charles, a straight-A prelaw senior whose father was a Dallas clothing tycoon. "Another girl on her floor said she'd gone off with you-know-who."

Cameron Dokey, another upperclass sister, added, "I actually saw KC and Marielle at McClaren Plaza. They were totally loaded. Everyone around was staring at them.

"We have to step in and stop this," Diane said. "Fast."

Courtney held up her hand. "I know. Believe me, I know. That's why we're all here." She looked from face to pretty face again. "I gave you all a little extracurricular assignment, the subject of which was our ex-sister Marielle Danner. Did any of you come up with anything?"

A few girls sheepishly shook their heads.

"We have to keep trying," Courtney said, trying not to look as worried as she felt. She'd assigned her trusted girls to investigate

Marielle. Courtney was looking for something—anything—that might give her some leverage over Marielle, and get Marielle away from KC. "We won't give up."

All the girls nodded glumly until Regina suddenly stood up. "We won't have to give up," she announced in her strong, twangy voice. "I think I've already found what we're looking for."

"Really?" Diane gasped. "Why didn't you say so?"

"I am saying so."

"Are you sure?" Courtney blurted, trying not to be overly optimistic.

Regina smiled. "I have the answer," she confirmed. She cleared her throat for dramatic effect. "I called home to see if my folks could find out anything."

"You called home?" Diane repeated, obviously confused.

"Yes. Marielle's parents live in Dallas now, too. And as we all know, her father is a very prominent attorney."

Courtney nodded. "So?"

"So," Regina went on, "according to my daddy, Mr. Danner wants to run for Congress. He not only wants to run, but he wants to win.

Part of his platform is none other than how he'll clean up the city's drug problem."

Courtney almost threw herself across the table to hug Regina.

Regina continued. "Anyway, the way I see it, Marielle's daddy isn't going to like it if everyone knows that the first druggie he needs to clean up is his own daughter."

All the girls began to smile.

"Do you have a plan?" Courtney asked.

"I think we just let Marielle know that we're onto her," Regina answered.

"How?" asked Diane.

Regina wasn't fazed. "We threaten to call her papa and tell him what we all know. And if Marielle doesn't leave KC alone after that, then I say we have my daddy call a few Dallas newspapers."

Regina looked as pleased as if she'd just put some horrible criminal away forever. "I think it will work. There're more than a few reporters in Dallas who'd love to print an article about how a future congressman's daughter spends her time at college leading other girls astray."

"I think it might work, too," Courtney said, feeling overwhelmingly relieved and grateful.

She knew that Regina's discovery was only a beginning. But it was the first ray of hope she'd had since KC had begun her downhill slide.

Seven

. . . .

M elissa stared in the mirror of Ella Day's Bridal Shop and couldn't believe that the person she saw reflected was really Melissa McDormand. "Do you think this fits right?" she asked, pivoting to the left and then to the right. The layers of white tulle and silk covering her body swooshed as she moved.

"You look fabulous," Faith assured her. She slithered out of her bridesmaid's dress, a vastly scaled-down version of the cloud of fabric that surrounded Melissa. "What do the rest of you think?"

Winnie got a quizzical look on her face. "Um, let's see, I'd say the dress makes Melissa"—she paused and laughed when she saw the stricken expression on Melissa's face—"breathtakingly beautiful."

"Absolutely," Lauren and Kimberly agreed.

All four girls stood around the mirror and stared. Ella Day's was on the Strand, the string of expensive shops in downtown Springfield. Brooks's family was sparing no expense on his wedding, and that included Melissa's dress, plus those for her bridesmaids.

Kimberly whacked at the hem of her dress. "I only have one complaint," she cracked. "My dress is too short. Maybe there's an extra-extra-long size I can try on."

"Or maybe we should all get our hems taken up to mini-skirt heaven," Winnie joked.

"How about if I just lengthen Kimberly's dress?" Ella Day said, coming over to check on the fitting. "Only the bride should make a big splash."

Melissa giggled. She was obviously having a great time being the center of attention, and looking at herself dressed like Princess Diana. She took a lacy veil from Ella Day and placed it on her head. Tears came to her eyes.

Faith and the other girls hovered around her. "Are you all right?" Faith asked.

"Don't start crying now," Kimberly warned, "or you'll get me started."

"Melissa, you do look beautiful," Lauren soothed.

Winnie kissed Melissa's cheek. "Cheer up. It'll all be over in a flash. I think that's the only way to get married. Josh thinks so, too. Just close your eyes, hold your breath, then presto— you're attached to another human for the rest of your life." She put her hands to her face. "Yikes."

"I just can't believe that all this is happening," Melissa confessed. She seemed softer than Faith had ever seen her. "Every day I get up and the wedding is one day closer, and more presents arrive from Brooks's relatives and friends. People keep calling to tell us they're coming. Brooks's parents have been super."

"They're nice, aren't they," Faith said.

Melissa nodded and looked right at her. Faith was suddenly embarrassed, realizing that she was the ex-girlfriend comforting the fiancée.

But Melissa seemed perfectly at ease. She ran her hands along her silk dress as if she still couldn't believe that she was wearing it.

"Brooks's mom calls me three times a day."

"Uh-oh," Kimberly warned. "A meddling mother-in-law."

"No way," Melissa said. "She's not a busybody. She's just excited and wants to help. She's already treating me like part of her family." She looked down at her dress again.

"Meanwhile nobody else can use our hall phone," Winnie joked.

Tears continued to roll down Melissa's face, but they were clearly tears of joy. "This is just all so perfect that I can't quite believe it." She looked back at her friends. "All of you. This dress. You know, I was so scared when Brooks and I tried to elope. And now I'm just getting more and more excited." She reached back and took Winnie's hand. "Don't any of you forget the wedding rehearsal on Saturday night."

"We won't," Winnie assured her.

Lauren and Kimberly reassured Melissa, too, but Faith had begun to back away. As she brushed against the racks of dresses, slips, and veils, she realized that she was truly happy for Melissa. Sure, she'd felt something a little strange when she'd kissed Brooks in the dining commons, but she didn't think it was anything more than a touch of nostalgia, a good-bye to the last big memory of high school.

"Melissa, lift your leg up. I want to try this garter on you."

"Winnie . . ."

"Look, you have to wear a garter or it won't be a real wedding."

Lauren giggled. "Winnie's right. I mean if we're going for this frilly stuff, then I say we go all the way."

"Yes, yes, yes," Kimberly chanted. She stood on the "modeling stool" Ella Day had placed before Melissa the minute they'd walked in. "And what about the bouquet! You know, Mel, you have to throw it. And whoever catches it gets married next." She tossed a hat to Winnie.

Winnie caught it, then pretended to balance it on her nose like a seal.

"Hey, I know you'll catch the bouquet," Faith called out from her position in the back of the store. "All that Frisbee practice you've had with Josh is going to pay off."

Faith suddenly realized that she was making her way toward the door and she wasn't sure why. It wasn't thoughts of Brooks or Melissa that were making her want to get out of the stuffy, perfumed bridal shop and into the open air. It was something else. The longer Faith watched Winnie and Lauren, Kimberly and Melissa having such a great time, the more strongly she felt that someone was missing. Even if Melissa and KC had never been super close, KC should have been there.

How could Melissa be so together, so optimistic, so happy, while KC was so mixed up, so wrung out, so depressed. It gave Faith a case of the shivers just thinking about it. She was actually trembling as if a ghost had passed by the shop.

"Oh my God," Faith whispered.

Her eyes shifted past the silk, the lace, the satin, and the fitting mannequin to the outside of the store window. She spotted KC walking by. No wonder she'd felt a ghostly presence.

Still peering through the shop window, Faith noticed how out of step KC seemed. Literally. KC was normally a shoulders-back, eyes-forward, chin-up kind of person. But that was not the person that Faith saw walk by. No, this was more like a phantom KC, a KC possessed. Her shoulders were hunched, not upright; her eyes downcast, not straight ahead; her step hesitant, not steady. Faith would have been more shocked except that she saw someone with KC—Marielle Danner. She remembered her promise to Courtney and cleared her throat.

"Um, I hate to tell you guys, but I think I'm having a caffeine attack," Faith blurted lamely. "I'm going to head down the Strand and see if I can find an espresso."

Laughter broke out. Winnie made cracks. Faith had been teased once or twice for being a coffee addict when she was trying to maintain her late-night theater schedule of running shows and doing rehearsals. Actually Faith wished that she used some other excuse, since the mention of any kind of addiction made her skin crawl.

"Bring me back a cup!" cried Winnie.

"Me too," Kimberly yelled.

Waving good-bye to all of them, Faith flew out the door of Ella Day's in hot pursuit of KC.

Halfway down the Strand Brooks was having an anxiety attack. It was so unlike him that he felt as if he had been jinxed. When he stopped at the crosswalk to wait for the light, his legs seemed to sway at the kneecaps. Brooks had experienced this while doing high-altitude mountain climbing but never in downtown Springfield. He was on his way to meet Melissa at the bridal shop, imagining himself as the white knight riding up on his horse. But suddenly all he saw was a black hole ready to swallow him up.

"I'm fine," Brooks blurted out as he continued to walk. "I'm more than fine. I'm great. *I'm getting married!*" he suddenly projected in full voice.

A kid on a bicycle riding past skidded to a halt, threw Brooks a look, then quickly pedaled off.

Brooks felt sheepish. He was overreacting. He was flipping out. Okay, so he'd woken up in the middle of the night in a cold sweat, filled with the memory of kissing Faith. Not Melissa. *Faith.*

That was normal, he told himself. It was the same as people on their deathbeds who saw their lives passing before their eyes. Guys getting married simply saw their ex-girlfriends flash before theirs. It didn't mean anything more. He still loved Melissa. He wanted to make *her* his life's partner. Wasn't that the truth?

Stop! he told himself. He touched his forehead. Maybe he was suffering from the onset of a virus, the beginning of a flu. Maybe the air downtown with all the traffic was too polluted.

He took shallow, rapid breaths, not the usual long, deep, supercharged balloon busters that were part and parcel of the mountain climber. That didn't seem to help, either. He was still woozy.

That's when Brooks noticed something funny. Across the street in Walker Park, hurrying, stopping, starting, and then taking cover behind a tree, was a young woman. Only this young woman was impossible not to notice, because she was the young woman who had been so totally on Brooks's mind.

"Faith," Brooks yelled out, even before he had time to think about it. When Faith looked at him, it was with an expression that immediately told Brooks that he had done something stupid. Nevertheless she began running toward him. She crossed the street and in a second was holding on to his arm.

"Hi, Brooks. Melissa is still in the bridal shop." She threw a glance down the street, as if she were following a robber or a murderer.

"So what are you doing here?" Brooks asked. He knew Faith well enough to be sure that she wasn't just out for an aimless stroll.

"Following KC."

"What about KC?"

An expression of pure pain swept over Faith's face. "She just walked by Ella Day's." Her voice suddenly cracked. "She's with Marielle."

"Marielle?"

"Marielle Danner," Faith said, in a voice that had now shifted to anger. "She lives in KC's dorm and she's gotten KC into drugs. I think they went into Walker Park."

Brooks had heard rumors about KC and Marielle. Still, he was surprised to hear Faith mention it so straightforwardly. "You saw them just now?"

"Just now," Faith went on. "I think they were headed for the topiary."

Now Brooks's stomach really went cuckoo. Everybody at the university knew that the topiary was a hangout for drug dealers, scuzbags, and lowlifes. "Great," he said.

"I know."

The pain on Faith's face made Brooks's heart ache. He began to feel even more light-headed. It wasn't like him to be confused by his feelings. It wasn't normal for him to feel like his emotions were one big crazy salad. He was nervous over his upcoming marriage. He was nostalgic over Faith. He was scared to death for KC, and he was suddenly angry at the world.

He decided to push the other feelings down and just go with the anger. At least with the anger he could do something. He could march into the park, confront KC, and drag her out kicking and screaming if he had to. That sounded like something a shining knight would do.

Faith seemed to be reading his mind in that old way she had when they'd been a couple. "Don't worry. I'm going to find her or at least see if I can find out what's going on," she told him. She put a hand on his chest.

He stared down at her pale fingers.

"But I don't want you to go with me. Melissa's waiting for you. And I don't want to alarm KC. Maybe she and Marielle just went in there for a walk."

Brooks gave Faith a disbelieving look. "Let me go with you," he insisted. "You need me."

Faith shook her head and pushed him back. "I can handle it. I'm just going to eavesdrop, Brooks. If I sense any danger, I'll come right out."

"You'll come right out and get me," he insisted.

She suddenly smiled at him. "Brooks, you're making this into some big thing, and it probably isn't. I know how you like to take care of people, but I'll be fine. Really."

Now Brooks was embarrassed. Faith had broken up with him because she felt that he was too overbearing and protective. "Okay." He sighed. "But if you ever do need me to help with KC—or anything—please let me know." He swallowed hard. "Just because I'm . . . getting married, doesn't mean I can't still be there for my old friends."

"Okay," Faith vowed, stepping closer to the park. She looked ahead of her, then turned back. "Go find Melissa. She looks beautiful."

"Right," Brooks muttered, realizing that he'd been thinking about how beautiful Faith looked. He started walking away from her. Then he called back. *"You let me know if you need me!"*

"I will," she called back.

Brooks watched her go and got that unsettled feeling again. As he strode toward the bridal shop he hoped that seeing Melissa would put everything in place again. If he could be Melissa's shining knight, maybe he wouldn't need to think about the other maidens in his life.

Eight

Hunted. Pursued. Hounded. That's how KC felt.

She'd seen Faith slip out of the bridal shop, stop and talk to Brooks, then follow her. It was time to run. She and Marielle sprinted into the damp, cold park and didn't stop until the sight of Brooks and Faith was just a memory.

"Whoa, I'm glad we got rid of those weirdos," Marielle said. "They would definitely have cramped our style."

KC hesitated. She suddenly wasn't sure why running away had seemed so all-important.

The answer, she knew, lay inside of herself, but she was too scared and too ashamed to look for it.

"Come on, KC," Marielle urged. "I told you I'd show you how to set this up. But I don't want to waste all day."

She was smoking a cigarette, even after all the running. A plaid scarf was twisted around her neck, and the hair that fell down one side was stuck to her mouth. Still, she didn't look scared. And she certainly didn't look ashamed.

But KC's stomach was still turning somersaults.

Why can't I just calm down? she asked herself for about the hundredth time. What was it about her lately that made the sky look bleached, the grass spiky, and the trees like giant green monsters? Even the hedges in the park looked ominous. The topiary was a maze of laurel hedges, all carved like something out of a cartoon or a crazy nightmare. Some were shaped like giant horses and dogs. They didn't seem like part of a landscape. Instead they were like bogeymen ready to jump out at her.

Still, Marielle led the way. She was obviously not intimidated by a bunch of overpruned plants. She obviously wasn't questioning her sanity. She had an appointment—a date that was KC's date as well.

"Hurry up," Marielle nagged.

KC moved faster.

The appointment was to take place in front of Whittaker Fountain. It was an old, corroded, green-stained thing empty of water and devoid of life except for thick scum that clung to the cupids on the surrounding walls. It always amazed KC that a fountain could get that slimy when it was in one of Springfield's best parks. It was almost as if everyone knew that the topiary attracted weirdos, so they just left that area to the degenerates and didn't bother to maintain it.

But there wasn't long to contemplate the fountain. Almost as soon as they arrived, a whistle pierced the cold air.

"Pssst . . . Marielle."

"Over here," she called.

"I'm coming," a male voice called back.

KC looked over to the right, where a tall, wraithlike figure blended inconspicuously with the green of the bushes.

"Jed," Marielle told KC. "He's my connection." She laughed and corrected herself. "I mean, *our* connection."

The shadow emerged. It belonged to a young man who was tall, rugged, and handsome, but furtive looking. He looked back and forth across the fountain, down the shrubby pathways, then finally his eyes suspiciously took in Marielle.

"You made it," Jed said.

"Of course we made it," Marielle answered back. She sauntered forward with a confidence that KC could only envy. There was something about this Jed guy that was handsome but dangerous at the same time. His leather jacket looked tough and dirty. His eyes never stayed in one place for long.

"We gonna make a deal?" Jed asked, without any other discussion. Suddenly he noticed KC and smiled broadly. He stuck his hands in his pockets and moved toward her. "I'd like to make a deal with you," he said. KC stiffened.

Jed looked back at Marielle. "Who's your friend?"

"This is KC," Marielle answered. She threw down the butt of her cigarette as if to signal that she, too, was ready for action. "Get to know her face, Jed, sweetie. If you play your cards right, she could become a very good customer."

Jed's eyes ran up and down KC's body. KC began to shake.

"Okay by me," Jed said, grinning.

"So what have you got?" Marielle asked him.

Jed reached into his pocket, and when his hand emerged, the palm was open to reveal some packets of powder and a hand-rolled cigarette. "What do you want?" he said slyly. "I have a pretty good supply."

Marielle whisked the rolled cigarette out of his palm, drew it appreciatively under her nose, then leaned in as Jed flicked out a lighter and ignited its tip. She breathed deep. "Mmm. Good," she said, when she finally exhaled. Then she casually reached back with the cigarette so that KC could sample it.

KC had been taking her share of pills since getting together with Marielle, and she'd even done coke once, but she'd never tried marijuana before.

Marielle waved the cigarette impatiently. "KC." She rolled her eyes. "Try it."

KC finally took it and like a robot put it to her lips and sucked in. The smoke stung like fire. Her eyes watered. The heat ripped at the back of her throat. "Uhhhh," she groaned. She began to cough as if her lungs would explode.

Jed and Marielle howled, as if KC's reaction were the funniest thing ever.

"Oh-oh." Marielle giggled, starting to gasp and drool. "It's an acquired taste—I guess."

"Where did you find this infant?" Jed said, referring to KC. He leaned on KC, until she moved away from him and he almost stumbled.

KC's head began to spin. The taste in her mouth was terrible, but all she was aware of now was that Jed was leering at her. She stared down at the path.

Jed held up the cigarette, then took another puff and held his breath. "So you want to buy some?" he asked, blowing smoke up into the sky.

"No thanks. Just tasting," Marielle said, flirting. "What KC and I are really into are ups and downs. Pills. You have any of those?"

Jed moved closer to KC and put his arm around her.

She froze.

"Unfortunately, I don't have any of those on me at the moment." He rubbed KC's shoulder. "But I could get some. If you're really nice."

Marielle giggled. "We're always nice."

"How about you?" Jed asked KC directly. "Are *you* nice?"

KC cringed. "Depends who I'm dealing with."

"Oh, that's a good one. I like you already."

Jed stroked KC's hair., "Shall we arrange to meet again?"

KC pulled away from him.

"You tell us when and where," Marielle said seriously. "Just give me time to collect some funds from the rest of my buddies. Try to get me forty uppers and forty downers."

Marielle was arranging to buy eighty pills! KC realized. She was practically getting to be a pusher herself.

"Okay." Jed looked around to make sure no one was coming. Then he pulled out an appointment book. "I can do that. But I need a few days. How about Saturday, at midnight."

"We'll be here," Marielle chirped. She linked her arm with KC's. "Both of us."

KC knew she was in over her head. She didn't want to be anywhere with Marielle and Jed ever again, but her brain was still cloudy from the dope and her mouth wouldn't work. Finally she thought of an excuse. "I can't come Saturday night," she said. "I have a sorority party."

Now Jed and Marielle began laughing hysterically. "I have a soroity party," Jed mimicked her. "La-di-da. Want me to come along and bring the party to life?"

KC swallowed and pushed Jed away.

"Okay, Miss Sorority Puss," Marielle said. "You go to your stupid Courtney kiss-up party, and then meet me at the entrance to this park. I'll slip you the cash, and then you can meet Jed and get our next supply."

"Me?" KC stuttered.

Marielle nodded. "We all have to learn sometime."

"Well, I mean . . . but . . . I . . ." KC didn't know what to say. She'd never done anything illegal before, at least not anything lawyers called "premeditated."

"So Saturday night it is," Jed said. He started to back away, clearly eager to meet another client who was winking him over. But before he left, he pushed himself up against KC again. "I look forward to seeing you, pretty face."

KC smiled feebly.

Jed stared at her, laughed again, then finally took off.

KC was still reeling from the feel and the stench of Jed, and the realization that she was actually going to make a buy, when she saw Marielle's eyes narrow.

"Hey! Who's there?" Marielle suddenly shouted.

"What?" KC mumbled.

"Someone's there!" Marielle said, pointing to a clump of nearby bushes.

KC watched with horror as the bushes rustled and shook. Someone was behind the hedge and possibly had been for some time. KC felt her stomach shrink as she envisioned a cop stepping out to arrest her. With a clutch in her throat she thought of her dying father learning that she'd been arrested for arranging to buy drugs.

But no cop appeared from behind the shrubbery. No narc or dealer or scum. Instead, Faith emerged, looking ashen and more worried than KC could ever remember.

"I know what's going on, KC," Faith immediately stated. "You're getting in way too deep."

"Who cares what you think?" Marielle spat out.

"I care," Faith shot back.

KC was still stunned to see her. She'd told herself over and over that her old friends had deserted her. She stared at Faith as if she were a ghost.

"Some caring," Marielle taunted. She flipped back a strand of limp hair. "From what KC tells me, all you care about is hoity-toity weddings and your goody-goody little morals."

"That's not true," Faith retorted. Her fair skin was red with anger, her eyes on the alert. "Maybe I'm not as sophisticated as you, Marielle, but KC is one of my oldest friends. You're bad news."

KC heard the words as if they were being played back on a droopy-sounding tape. Oh, yeah! she felt like yelling. Oh yeah! Where were you when I needed you.

"Oh yeah?" KC finally heard herself say.

But when she looked back at Faith, she felt much less sure. Faith's eyes were swimming in worry. Meanwhile Marielle just watched, as she often did when she found a situation interesting.

"KC, don't let Marielle use you like this," Faith pleaded. "She's going to destroy you. Please let me help. I'm your friend. You're in terrible trouble."

Trouble?

KC heard the word and felt a surge of anger cut through the haze of confusion, stupor, and doubt that had been clouding her brain. Where were you when I was really in trouble? she asked herself. Where were you and Winnie when Peter went away? Or when things got rough at the sorority? Heck, where were you when I even wanted to join the sorority? Where was everyone when my father got sick?

"You don't know what you're talking about," KC shouted.

Marielle grinned.

"Yes, I do," Faith insisted. "And the KC I know knows it, too."

But KC wasn't backing down. "I'm telling you this is none of your business, and I don't appreciate you following me around like some kind of spy."

"Me either," Marielle chimed in.

Faith's eyes suddenly filled with tears. For a moment KC thought it was just the cold, but she could hear the shakiness in Faith's voice and then it was clear it wasn't the temperature.

"KC, please. I love you," Faith pleaded. "I'm here for you. Whatever problems you're having can be worked out. I'll do anything to help. But please . . . listen to me. You're going to make a mistake that could ruin your whole life."

"Maybe I want to ruin my whole life," KC insisted.

"That's right, it's her life, anyway," Marielle broke in. "So why don't you just go and mess with somebody else's head? We didn't ask you to follow us here."

Faith obviously couldn't think of anything else to say.

KC was caught for a few more seconds. But finally she linked arms with Marielle.

"See you later," KC sang to Faith. "And you better hurry out of the park before dark. Otherwise some nasty people might pop out of the bushes and get you."

Faith stood there, stunned.

KC didn't look back. Marielle urged her forward, and they raced off into the park.

Nine

"I can't believe you own so much stuff," Kimberly told Lauren the next morning.

"*I* can believe it," Lauren complained as she dropped her end of her stereo onto Forest Hall's basement floor. "Thanks for helping me move. I could never have done this alone."

"We still have a long ways to go," Kimberly said, as she propped up one speaker against a post.

Both girls sighed. They looked around at the dorm storage area. Skis, bikes, a canoe, lamps, dozens of cardboard boxes, and mountains of other junk had found their way down here. The storage area looked like a cross between the world's biggest junk sale and somebody's huge messed-up closet.

"It's all those moms," Kimberly suddenly decided.

"What?" Lauren didn't think she had heard her right.

"Yeah, moms. You know how they always think you haven't brought enough blankets, or you need more hangers, or that you just can't live without the hideous old lamp in the garage that Aunt Milly gave you."

Lauren smiled. "Actually, my theory is that by sending this stuff off with their kids to college, the parents are secretly cleaning up their own house."

"No kidding. You should see how my old bedroom back home is now. I mean, I don't even recognize it. My mom has even given it a new name —the *sewing* room. Of course when I lived there you could hardly walk in it, but still . . ."

Lauren was feeling good enough to laugh. Just the act of moving her stereo and journals felt like a new start. And she couldn't imagine that Kimberly would have ever had a bedroom that was a disaster area. Now, her own room back with her parents had always been super-neat. But that was because the maid had cleaned it every day.

"You ready to go again?" Kimberly asked.

Lauren wiped the perspiration from her brow. Her legs felt less wobbly, her face less flushed. She could even face the prospect of reclimbing the Forest Hall stairway knowing that she might get hit with water balloons thrown by some demented jock. "Absolutely. Let's go."

Kimberly slipped between a bulletin board and an old dresser. As usual she looked lithe, even energetic. She was the perfect moving partner, because she just kept going.

Up the steps they went. The Jeep was empty and Lauren couldn't wait to fill it up again. It was almost as if she wanted to erase every memory of her shabby off-campus room and start over as Winnie's roommate. Forest Hall, here I come, Lauren thought.

They both got in and drove past the sororities and fraternities on Greek Row, past the big, old student boardinghouses that lined the hills on Seventeenth street, past the campus bookstore and record shops and student hangouts. Lauren could almost taste the coffee in the espresso shops and hear the records in the record stores. She was honestly relieved to be moving back on campus. She'd missed the gossip and giggles, the camaraderie and late-night talks. When she'd first arrived at U of S, she'd lived in Coleridge Hall with Faith. That was before Dimitri, before Dash. So now she was going full circle, moving back into the dorms with Faith's old friend Winnie.

They turned off Maple Avenue and down the street of what would soon be Lauren's former address. Lauren began to slow her Jeep down so she could park, when out of the corner of her eye she spotted a male figure walking up to the front door of her old building.

Without thinking, Lauren pushed her foot down hard on the gas.

"Lauren!" Kimberly protested. "We're going past your apartment!"

"I forgot something," Lauren lied.

"What could you possibly have forgotten? We're moving you into Forest Hall, remember, not out of it."

"Just believe me, Kimberly," Lauren insisted. "I . . . I . . . I just forgot something, okay?"

Kimberly looked at her with an expression of pure puzzlement. "Okay," she said in a resigned voice. "Whatever you say."

Lauren was glad Kimberly didn't press her, because she wasn't sure what she was going to do. But as if her Jeep were being pulled around the block like a magnet, she found herself driving right back to her apartment. This time her eyes were glued to the front stoop. Sure enough, it was Dash standing there.

She stared at him, every detail stamping itself in her brain—his red bandanna, the scruffy blue jeans, the long hair, the day-old growth of beard. Lauren found herself feeling like her heart had just dribbled down her chest.

"Did you invite *him* over?" Kimberly gasped. She leaned forward and stared at Dash, too. "Now I see why you flipped out. How long has it been since you've seen each other?"

"Not that long," Lauren answered. Her confusion and panic wasn't due to the fact that she hadn't seen Dash recently, but rather to the crossing emotions she felt for him. And she didn't know how to untangle them.

"What do you think he wants?"

Lauren pulled the Jeep over and turned off the engine. She took a deep breath. Dash was on the porch, but he'd heard the Jeep and was now looking at them. Weeks of decision, of resolve, of discipline and heartache flooded Lauren's brain. Why, why, why had he come around? she thought. He'd known all about Dimitri. Actually, he'd been the one to warn her—although she'd tried hard not to believe him.

Kimberly folded her long arms. She shook her head. "Well, I don't think he's here to sell you a newspaper subscription." She laughed, but Lauren didn't.

Instead, they both got out of the Jeep. Lauren slammed her door as hard as possible. She wasn't quite sure why, but it made her feel better.

"Lauren!" Dash called out.

"Dash," Lauren said in a barely audible voice.

They both walked fast toward each other, as if for some reason they were in a great big hurry.

"Glad I caught you," Dash said. He smiled and seemed cool, although Lauren noticed that he was rocking on his heels.

"Hi," Kimberly piped up.

Dash lifted a finger to acknowledge her. "You're moving, huh?"

"Yeah," Lauren answered, with no further explanation. She pushed her hands into the pockets of her parachute pants, then looked down at the ground.

Kimberly watched both of them.

"Well, uh, I had to talk to you about this," Dash said in a voice that meant he wasn't sure what he was doing there. Nonetheless he held up a sheaf of typing paper. It was obviously a story that had been submitted to the *Weekly Journal*, the campus newspaper. Lauren instantly recognized her own editorial comments smeared all over the margins of the text.

"Is that Jamie Harris's story?" she asked.

"Yes."

"I edited the copy just like I was supposed to," Lauren answered, referring to the task assigned to her the week before. Lately the newspaper had wanted more experienced writers to help newcomers by editing the first drafts of their articles.

Dash nodded. "Um, well, I didn't agree with all of your notes. But I think they'll help Jamie."

"Good. You didn't have to come all the way here to tell me that."

Dash shifted. He didn't really look at her, and he wasn't really looking at the newspaper article, either. In fact, Lauren couldn't tell where he was looking.

"Is there anything else?" she asked hopefully. "I mean, having to do with the newspaper."

By this time Kimberly had walked a few yards away and was examining the sidewalk as if she'd lost a hundred-dollar bill.

"Well, I . . ." Dash mumbled.

Suddenly Lauren was moved at the sight of cocky Dash, charming unflappable Dash, stuttering like a kid at his first cotillion. "Dash, is that all?" she prompted.

He stuck his hands in his pockets. "Not really. But, well, maybe this isn't a good time. I mean, I didn't know you were moving and everything."

She realized that she didn't want him to leave. "Well, if it's important."

"It is, but we can talk later."

"Are you sure?"

"Yes. We'll talk some other time."

Kimberly finally came back. "*Lauren*, we've got all that stuff to move," she said in an exasperated tone. "Or should I go away and come back."

Dash's face suddenly flushed red, but no redder than Lauren's. Her heart had sped up and her knees felt like Jell-O.

"I guess we can talk on Monday," she said. "At our breakfast meeting."

"Yeah, right. I don't mean to hold you up. Go ahead with Kimberly and move."

They looked at each other for several long seconds before shifting their gazes.

Kimberly tugged at Lauren's arm. "Let's go."

"Okay."

"Bye," Dash said.

Lauren just nodded. Then in a minute he was gone.

The two girls walked into the rooming house. Silently they went about their work. They tugged, pulled, piled, unpiled, loaded, and pushed. In half an hour they had the Jeep packed again. Neither one of them said a word about Dash, which was fine with Lauren.

When they got back to campus, the only parking space they could find was several blocks from the dorm. Still, they hauled a big box full of books out of the Jeep. What they hadn't counted on was how much heavier the box got with each step. About the third time they'd put the box down on the sidewalk to rest and restore their aching backs and arms, Lauren noticed Kimberly staring out across the grassy playing field where a touch-football game was going on.

"What is it?" Lauren asked.

"Look."

Lauren looked and realized that she was searching for Dash. But then she got it. *Derek!* Kimberly had spotted Derek. He was in the midst of running, jumping, and flying after the football.

"Ugh," Kimberly said. "Why does he have to be here? He's the last person I want to see."

Lauren nodded. She felt a little better now that Kimberly was being haunted by *her* old boyfriend, just as she was being haunted by Dash.

Hauling, pushing, carting, dragging, and grunting, they finally made it to Forest Hall. And that was just the first of several times they traipsed back and forth with Lauren's belongings. Each time Derek looked their way, but he continued to play football.

Lauren thought he might at least say something to her, perhaps even offer to help carry the heavier boxes.

But nooooooooooo . . .

Derek was ignoring them. He was being an incomprehensible blockhead, just like Dash, just like the whole male half of the human race. By the time they were finally done with carrying everything into the basement, Lauren wasn't sure whether she was exhausted at moving all the stuff or exhausted from being so mad at guys!

"Let's go to my dorm and listen to some music," Kimberly suggested as they walked by Derek and the rest of the football players. "I'm not going to let Derek's immature behavior get me down anymore."

"Okay."

When they got to Kimberly's door in Coleridge Hall, they both stopped and stared. A pink envelope was taped to her door, along with a foil balloon that bobbed slightly.

"Not another one!" Kimberly railed. She punched the balloon, then ripped the envelope off. Inside was a typed note. Kimberly read it quickly, then handed it to Lauren.

Dear Kimberly:

Once again I have to admit that you are the most intelligent, beautiful, and extraordinary person on campus. Why won't you come to your senses and be with me?

"*Can you believe this!*" Kimberly screamed, shaking her head. "He won't talk to me in the dining commons. He won't help us move a box, but then he leaves notes and doesn't even have the nerve to sign his name."

Lauren stared at the note. "It is kind of weird," she admitted. "I don't quite get it."

Kimberly threw up her hands. "You and me both. Derek wants to come across as a macho stud, so he ignores my existence, and then he expects me to come crawling back to him! Never! Not crawling, walking, or standing on my head." She grabbed the note back and began ripping it into tiny pieces.

Lauren nodded in understanding. She thought about Dash. She thought about Dimitri. She thought about Kimberly and Derek. She thought about how impossible it seemed for the two sexes to work things out.

"I'm beginning to believe men and women don't belong on the same planet," she said softly.

Ten

··········

On Friday afternoon it was raining heavily on the Springfield campus. Yet even though Courtney didn't have classes or appointments forcing her to venture out in the downpour, she strode across McClaren Plaza with purpose. Today she was going to put a stop to someone, someone she'd wanted to put a stop to long ago.

So she ducked into Howard Hall and waited outside Room 360.

At ten to eleven the door finally swung open. Students started wandering out. Courtney nodded to a few people she knew and smiled back at several guys who paused to smile at her. Finally the girl she was waiting for slumped out of the class.

"Marielle."

Marielle looked up as if she'd been caught stealing stockings from her older sister. Her eyes looked tired and circled. Her skin was a pasty white, and her lips chapped and pale. She looked frighteningly thin in a leotard and a pair of skintight jeans. Her posture was slumped and suggestive of low energy, until she saw Courtney. Then she grew rigid and defensive looking.

"What do *you* want?" Marielle asked in her southern drawl.

"I want to talk to you," Courtney answered curtly.

"I'm not one of your little sisters anymore," Marielle challenged. "I don't have to talk to you."

Courtney stood her ground. "I think you'll want to talk to me when you hear what I have to say."

Marielle seemed to want to walk away, but she wasn't quite able to. She got out of the traffic and leaned against the wall. "So talk," she said snottily.

Courtney didn't mince words. "I don't like the way you're getting revenge on me through KC. I want you to leave KC alone."

"Buzz off." Marielle sneered as she tried to get past Courtney. "You're such an egomaniac. You think everything in the world has to do with you and your stupid sorority."

Courtney pinned her to the stair rail. "I'm serious," she said, anger rising in her tone. "I will not stand by and let you ruin KC's life."

Marielle let out a forced laugh. "HA. That's really funny coming from you. You're the one who's ruined her life, you and all her phony sorority sisters."

"You're just bitter because the Tri Betas kicked you out," Courtney shot back. "But you didn't get anything you didn't deserve. And now, if you want to throw your life away, go ahead. I don't care what happens to you anymore. But I will not let you take someone I care about with you."

Marielle scowled. "Courtney, I didn't know you cared about anyone."

"Well, that just proves that you don't know much, Marielle—and that's something I always suspected." Courtney stepped back a little. She was starting to feel dirty just standing next to

Marielle. "Look, we don't need to chat for long. What I have to say to you is very simple."

Marielle batted her eyes. "Yes, Miss Courtneee," she drawled.

Courtney glared at her. "Here's the deal, Marielle. You leave KC alone, or else."

Marielle started to giggle. "Or else? What is this, some kind of Mafia movie? Courtney and the Tri Beta family?" She laughed harder. "Or else what, Courtney? Are you going to come to my dorm room with your hit man and shoot me?"

Courtney took a deep breath.

Marielle kept talking. "Has it ever occurred to you, Courtney, that KC and I might have a lot in common? Instead of putting pressure on her, or making her live up to some holier-than-thou, uptight image of a sorority sister, I just want her to be herself, to loosen up, and yes, maybe even to have fun."

"I see," Courtney spat back. "Is that what drugs are called? Fun?"

Marielle smiled snidely. "Courtney, you wouldn't know fun if it bit you in the butt. You don't know anything about drugs, and you don't know anything about KC."

Courtney felt a sudden rush of tears. "I know

what my brother looked like after being addicted to cocaine for two years. And believe me, Marielle, it was not a pretty sight."

Finally Marielle shut up. She bit her lip and looked off, pretending to be bored.

Courtney stood even straighter. "Look, I don't want to stand here with you any longer than I have to, Marielle. So I'm just going to tell you one thing. Do you remember Regina Charles?"

Marielle pushed her nose up. "Another Tri Beta snob queen, a bore, a straight-A ice bucket."

"Well, that straight-A ice bucket," Courtney repeated, "just happens to come from Dallas, where your father now lives."

"My father?" Marielle gasped. Finally the impudence left her wasted face.

"Your father," Courtney repeated. "I believe he's running for Congress down there and wants to win something fierce."

Marielle drew in a sharp breath. "What about him?"

Courtney laid out her plan very matter-of-factly. "Well, my guess is that your father has no idea about what his precious daughter is into these days. But he will soon, and so will the rest of Dallas . . . unless you leave KC alone."

"What are you saying?" Marielle said slowly.

Courtney smiled. "I'm saying that if you don't stop talking to, hanging out with, supplying and in any other way damaging KC with your friendship, the Dallas newspapers will be told every detail the Tri Betas know about your drug use. I'm sure all of Dallas will find it fascinating breakfast reading, especially in light of your father's political ambitions. Don't you agree?"

Marielle's skin grew even paler. She brushed her limp hair out of her eyes, looked down at the ground, and for a moment appeared to be on the verge of getting sick. Finally her words squeaked out. "You wouldn't," she said.

Courtney nodded, her eyes steely and focused. "Try me. You know that I don't bluff."

Marielle flinched, but this time there was no smart comeback. For once she kept her eyes lowered and her mouth closed.

Satisfied that Marielle finally understood, Courtney released her, walked down the stairs, and back out into the rain.

"Is this going to be a wedding party or what? Are we really doing something this corny!"

"Win, nobody's here yet. You could be a little quieter."

"Not in this dorm," Winnie cracked. "In this dorm I'm just warming up."

Brooks clapped a hand over Winnie's mouth and interrupted her silly answer. She broke up in giggles. Her dorm room was decorated to the hilt and she, Brooks, and Melissa were waiting for the guests to arrive.

Winnie could hardly believe Brooks and Melissa were truly going to get married that Sunday. However, it was a great excuse to have another party, so she had gone all out for the patented Gottlieb antishower shower. Now if Brooks would just let her talk again and the guests would arrive, she could get the whole thing started.

Winnie brushed Brooks's hand away. "I wanna talk," she said loudly, then she giggled again.

Melissa shushed them both. She had so many last-minute phone calls to make that Lauren had loaned her a portable telephone to use in the room. She was on with Brooks's mother, trying to concentrate on the umpteen million details of the wedding. In spite of all the madness, she looked radiantly happy. Her cheeks were pink, her red hair as healthy looking as a carrot, her eyes quick, alert, and loving. Winnie thought she looked like a person on a wonderful wild ride who never wanted it to stop.

"I think your idea about the flowers is wonderful," Melissa said into the phone. She nudged Brooks, who was looking at the pile of antishower shower presents. On Winnie's bed were the formal wedding presents, which had been arriving daily in the mail. Winnie figured that if any more presents arrived, she'd have to move in with Josh.

"I'll tell the florists tomorrow night at the rehearsal," Melissa said. "When will you get in?"

"My folks arrive tomorrow morning," Brooks called to her. Then he reached for one of the presents.

Winnie slapped Brooks's hand. "No peeking ahead of time. Some of these are just rewrapped from the shower that we didn't have before, but don't worry, some are new. Like the soap shaped like an artichoke and the gummy worms."

Brooks tried to laugh, but Winnie noticed that he didn't seem nearly as relaxed as Melissa now. It was almost as if he and Melissa had gone through some brain–body exchange. Well, maybe that's what happened when people got married.

"When is this thing supposed to get going?" Brooks asked nervously.

"Pretty soon. We're just waiting for a few more people."

As if on cue, there was a knock at the door. Lauren, Faith, and Kimberly stepped in with Barney Sharfenburger, Brooks's roommate. Their arms were full of packages, and they wasted no time in hustling over to the present pile and making a deposit.

Brooks looked at Faith, then quickly looked away.

Melissa said good-bye to Brooks's mom and put down the phone. She immediately ran over and gave hugs to Faith, Kimberly, and Lauren. "Thanks for coming," she said.

"Are you kidding?" Kimberly batted one of the orange-and-black Halloween balloons that for some reason Winnie had chosen for the party. "We wouldn't have missed this for the world. I mean, when Winnie does one of her weird parties, you just know it's going to be something."

"Yeah," Winnie answered, stretching her arms up to show off a black leotard under her orange

T-shirt outfit that matched perfectly with the antishower shower decorations. "I found all these Halloween items on sale downtown," she explained. "I thought that it would be a nice contrast to all the pink ribbons and stuff you normally see at showers."

"Does this mean getting married is supposed to scare me to death?" Brooks joked in a stiff voice.

Melissa came over and threw her arms around his neck and then sat down on his lap. "I'm the marriage monster," she said, giggling.

"Some monster," Brooks teased, pulling away from her slightly. "How were the real monsters, my family?" He glanced at Faith again.

Faith smiled, but didn't say anything.

Melissa looked quietly satisfied. "They're great. Your cousins, your uncle Max, and your aunt Dolly are arriving tomorrow morning, too."

Kimberly pretended to fan herself. "Brooks, you never told us you had an Aunt Dolly."

"Yeah, well," Brooks stammered. "There's a lot you don't know."

Melissa grinned and kissed him. "Brooks's family is terrific," she announced. "Even my family is acting fairly human about this. I mean, you know things are going well when *my* family is being supportive."

Winnie couldn't believe it. She hadn't seen her act this positive since Melissa had looked forward to the dissecting section of her anatomy class. Winnie waved her arms and suddenly made an announcement. "In just a few ghoulish minutes I'm going to cut a pumpkin pie. And of course there will be a plastic bride and groom sitting on top. I do have to stick the candles in, however."

"Candles?" Lauren wondered.

"Yeah, about a hundred and fifty of them. One for every year Brooks and Melissa are going to be happily married."

There was more laughter. Winnie looked at all the happy faces and realized somebody was missing. And it just happened that the missing face belonged to her own great love, Josh.

"Be right back. I've got to run down the hall and check that the soda machine is all stocked up," she said quickly. "I hate to be tacky, but if we run out of my special orange party punch, we may have to resort to quarters and soda, so drink responsibly, guys."

Winnie's joke brought another laugh, but people were beginning to get curious about the presents. Winnie had the chance now to simply step outside her door, walk down the hall, and check out what was happening with Josh.

As she walked out into the hallway she tried to remember if Josh had said he'd be late. She couldn't. So why wasn't he at the party?

Winnie took a deep breath in front of Josh's door. Then she knocked, but didn't wait for an answer before she twisted the doorknob. "Hello," she said as she burst in.

Josh was hunched over his computer, tapping away, in that never-never land of electronic glare that told Winnie he was doing a nerdy Josh space-out. Her heart froze. Was this the old Josh coming back? He promised never to do this to her again!

"Hello," Winnie repeated.

Josh still didn't turn around. That's when Winnie noticed that he had his Walkman on. She marched over and tugged at the collar of his sweatshirt.

"Hello again!" she yelled out.

Josh just about jumped out of his chair.

"Hi," he stammered, taking off the head-phones. "You sure know how to scare a person."

"Well, good. Now what is going on?" Winnie

almost yelled. "I mean, this is only the second time I've thrown this shower. First Melissa and Brooks didn't show up, now you."

Josh rubbed his eyes. "I'm sorry, Win."

"I thought we'd discussed this. I thought we'd come to some kind of understanding." Winnie's voice cracked and she suddenly felt weak with emotion. She wandered over to Josh's roommate, Mikoto's, side of the room and sat down on his bed.

Josh came over to put an arm around her, but Winnie threw him a look that said "back off," so he leaned against a night table.

"I didn't mean to forget," Josh insisted. "I'm just finishing my history paper. It's almost done."

"Great, Josh. You know, if I had a list of all the times you've forgotten to show up since we've been together, it would be longer than a graduate student's reading list."

Josh laughed, but Winnie wasn't trying to be funny, so he got quiet again. Then he shrugged and went over to the other side of the room and sat down on his bed across from Winnie. "What can I say? I screwed up. I should have finished last night, but I played computer games with Mikoto."

"You did what?" Winnie felt herself starting to cry. If this started happening again, she didn't know what she would do. But she loved Josh so much now that the thought of doing something hurtful and crazy filled her with dread. She began to get up from the bed, but Josh reached out and held her by the arm.

"Wait, Win. I'm sorry."

"Josh. You promised me you wouldn't be a spaced-out nerd anymore. But it seems like you're spaced out and nerdier than ever."

"I know. But I wasn't spending last night just nerding out with Mikoto. He and I found out about that climbing shop in Nevada where they sell those crampons Brooks wants. I thought you and I could drive there tomorrow night after the wedding rehearsal, then come back with them in time for Mel and Brooks's wedding."

The expression on Winnie's face said that she hadn't quite comprehended Josh's words. "What?"

"You know, the wedding present we talked about getting them. The crampons for climbing."

Winnie suddenly realized that she didn't want him to explain anymore. So Josh got nerdy once in a while. She was hardly perfect. So he even missed important events and tuned her out. What mattered was that he thought of others, like Melissa and Brooks. And when Winnie needed him, he was always right there.

She suddenly jumped up from the bed and threw her arms around Josh. He fell backward and she began kissing and hugging him like a puppy. "Oh Josh, what am I getting uptight about? I don't want you to flunk history and I don't care if you're late to some dorky party. I love you, do you know that?"

Josh pulled her in and held her tight. "Most of the time." He sighed.

"Well, know it all the time," Winnie told him. "Because I love you all the time, even when you're hunched over your computer playing Crystal Quest. Don't ask me why, but I do."

Josh pulled back and touched her face. The love in his eyes almost made her swoon. He kissed her mouth, her cheek, the hollow of her neck. "Funny thing, Win," he whispered. "I just happen to feel the same way about you."

Eleven

Brooks looked around the reception room of the Springfield Country Club and tried for the umpteenth time to convince himself that this wedding rehearsal was just that. Practice. A rehearsal. For the real thing.

Everything was set up: the banquet tables, the flower stands, the PA system and stage for the band, the red carpet that threaded its way down between two separate sections of chairs—one for Brooks's guests and one small section for Melissa's—the raised steps and platform where the carpet ended, the dais where they would actually recite their vows.

"Brooks, would you please step over here."

"Where?"

"Over here, right next to your bride-to-be."

It was the voice of Canon Harcourt, who was performing at the wedding. Thoughtful, steady, reassuring, he had come up from Jacksonville with Brooks's parents. He'd known Brooks since Brooks was a kid, and at the moment he was rehearsing the vows with just Melissa and Brooks. The rest of the wedding party was waiting outside in the foyer.

Melissa moved in very close to Brooks. She was in jeans and a T-shirt, but she looked as radiant as if she were already in her wedding dress.

Brooks saw her glow, but didn't feel her warmth, even with her standing right next to him. Instead he was feeling like a knight who'd fallen off his horse and wasn't quite sure how to get back up. He felt jittery as if his feet weren't quite planted on the ground.

"Sorry," he blurted, bumping into Melissa.

Melissa smiled at him. "That's okay."

Suddenly Brooks wanted to drag her out of the country club and just talk to her. He wanted to tell her about all the confusing dreams and feelings he'd been having lately.

Between all the plans and fittings, the picking people up at the airport, the parties and presents, he and Melissa had barely had any normal time alone together. She was starting to look like a stranger. He reminded himself how wonderful she was, how crazy he was about her, and how great it was that his parents and her parents had pulled together for the wedding. But it was as if all the good things about their relationship, all the love and respect between them, had poured out and filled up the lives of their families and friends.

He clasped his hand around Melissa's.

Melissa almost jumped. "Brooks, your hand is so cold."

His hands *were* ice cold, almost as if he were getting sick. He was pale, and unsteady.

"Are you all right?" Melissa asked him.

"What's that?" Canon Harcourt answered instead.

"Oh, I'm sorry," Melissa said, "I was just asking Brooks a question."

Now Canon Harcourt looked at Brooks. He folded the notebook with all the rehearsal notes and set it to his side. "Young man, from the looks of things I think all of us could use a

break," he said, smiling. "We have been at this
for a while. How about if we rest for ten minutes, and then reassemble here up on the dais,
before we go through the rest of the ceremony
with everyone again."

Brooks's eyes closed and then reopened, and
finally a single word came out. "Yes."

Melissa continued to hold his hand, but
Brooks didn't look at her, even when the two of
them turned around. Then they could see
Canon Harcourt wave the crowd in again. All
the people started to assemble behind them—
Winnie, Faith, Lauren, Kimberly, Barney, Josh—
Brooks's mom and dad, his high-school soccer
coach, his childhood best friend, Billy O'Toole,
even Aunt Dolly, who'd flown in early to attend
the rehearsal.

Melissa leaned into him. She slipped her arm
around his waist. Then they descended the pair
of steps down to the aisle of red carpet.

At the bottom they were met by their dorm
friends.

"Wow, is this a lot to go through," Winnie
said excitedly, "but I really like Canon
Harcourt." She was wearing pants that seemed
to be made of foil wrapping paper, plus a T-
shirt that said, *Just visiting this planet.*

"The minister's a definite dude," added Josh. Then he tickled and kissed Winnie. "I like this marriage bit."

"It's going to be really nice," Faith chimed in. She met Brooks's eyes and something seemed to pass between them. But then she deflected it with a punch to his shoulder. "How are you, Brooks? You look a little nervous."

"So do you," he heard himself say.

Faith looked embarrassed and pretended not to have heard him.

Brooks finally nodded to Melissa, as if nothing odd had happened. "I guess I am nervous," he admitted. "A little."

"Well, you haven't done this before," Lauren joked. She was wearing army pants and a linen blouse with a carnation pinned to it. "Actually, I've never been a bridesmaid before, either."

"It's just so strange," Brooks said vaguely.

"I hope it's not me that's strange." Melissa laughed. "Not that I want to be Miss Average."

Brooks inched away from her, but she held him more tightly. He stroked his face a little groggily, as if he were trying to wake up. "Yeah, I guess it's just nerves. This isn't something a person does every day."

"I hope not," Faith stated.

She met his eyes again, but this time he tried not to get stuck on her gaze.

"If I did this every day," Winnie acknowledged, "I definitely wouldn't invite this many people."

Brooks looked back at the crowd of relatives ambling around the room, examining the decor and presents that had been brought over. He waved to his uncle Harold, who'd flown in all the way from Chicago. Melissa waved to his mom. Then Brooks caught his father's eye and got a big, proud smile. "It looks like just about everybody's here," Brooks murmured, almost to himself.

"You know, *some* people were invited but didn't show up," Kimberly suddenly said, in a miffed tone of voice. She folded her arms over her chest in a disgusted gesture.

Lauren frowned. "You don't mean Derek, do you?"

Kimberly shrugged. "Who else?"

"He had a fencing meet," Brooks explained. Actually, he was glad to have one less person there. Each new arrival made him feel more and more pressured. "He called me to apologize."

"Well, he's been known to get a little flaky at crucial times," Kimberly said. "Not exactly someone you can depend on."

"Kimberly," Lauren interrupted, "this is a wedding rehearsal. We're supposed to be joyous."

Kimberly nodded. "I know. I just wish Derek would find better things to do with his time than bug me with dumb notes. I got another one this morning. And I intend to talk to him about it tomorrow."

"Okay, everybody!" Canon Harcourt called out. "Time to add the rest of our wedding party and go through this one more time. Then we can all go home and get some sleep before the real ceremony."

There were claps and some cheers. Everybody waited for Canon Harcourt to tell them where to stand—everybody but Brooks. When he'd heard the minister's words, he'd headed off in the opposite direction.

"Brooks, where are you going?" Melissa called after him.

"I need a drink of water."

Brooks hurried down the hallway. He wasn't exactly sure where he was going, but he knew there had to be a drinking fountain around here somewhere. His head was spinning. When he heard footsteps following behind him, he

turned into the nearest door available. It happened to be a swinging door, one that led into
the country-club kitchen.

"Hey, man, watch it!"

"Sorry," Brooks muttered.

There was that word again. *Sorry*. Sorry for
this, sorry for that. Were you supposed to be
that sorry about getting married and trying to
get through your own wedding? Shining knights
didn't bumble and apologize. And this time
Brooks really did need to be sorry, because he'd
walked into the path of an oncoming busboy,
and only the busboy's quick reflexes had pre-
vented a major disaster.

The busboy clapped a hand on a dish that was
still spinning on a tray. "You need something?"

"I was wondering where I could get a drink
of water."

"Hey, no problem."

The busboy darted off. In a second he
returned with a full glass. Brooks gulped it
down. But instead of feeling better, he suddenly
felt worse—like he might throw up or pass out.
The busboy stared at him.

"You okay?"

"Yeah."

"Guess you're the groom?"

Brooks barely nodded.

The busboy pointed. "I think some people out there are calling for you. Hang in there."

"Right." Brooks had heard the voices. He thanked the busboy, turned back around, walked down the hall into the reception and back into his wedding rehearsal.

"There you are," Melissa said, her voice still upbeat, her smile straightforward, her beautiful face open and happy for everyone to see.

"Sure. Sorry," he said again. "Just needed a drink of water."

Brooks remounted the dais, then once more took Melissa's hand. She flinched slightly at his touch, but said nothing more about his body temperature.

The rehearsal went faster this time. People seemed to have a better sense of what to do. Brooks was amazed that no one tripped, stuttered, dropped anything, or spaced out. He was even more amazed that *he* didn't do any of those things, but he seemed to be more together now. When Canon Harcourt finally closed his book, there were big smiles all around.

Brooks and Melissa walked down the stairs again. The first two people to meet them were Winnie and Josh. Both beamed. They were

clinging to one another like vines. Brooks had
the sudden thought that that's how he and
Melissa should have looked.

"We hate to rehearse and run," Winnie joked.
She gave Josh a grin. "But we have to go."

Josh shook Brooks's hand. "We're going
somewhere tonight, Brooks, so if you get the
three A.M. jitters, don't call me."

Winnie wrapped herself even more lasciviously
around Josh. "And we're not telling you where
we're going. It's a surprise."

Josh leaned in. "We're getting your wedding
present," he admitted. "We'll be back in time to
see the real thing tomorrow. You're a brave
man."

Brooks didn't feel brave as he watched Josh
and Winnie rush out, ahead of everyone. And
he didn't want to think about presents. Each
present that arrived just made him feel as if
another weight was being placed on his head.

Brooks was feeling really thirsty again.
Parched. He headed back to the kitchen where
he hoped he could beg another glass of water.
Melissa started to follow him, but was headed
off by his mother, who wanted her to meet
some more relatives who had just arrived from
out of town.

That's when he saw Faith, standing alone outside the kitchen. His heart flipped over and he rushed to join her.

"Are you really all right?" she asked as soon as she saw him. There was a new directness in her eyes, as if she'd been hiding something in front of the others, too.

Brooks had the craziest, most terrifying impulse to throw his arms around her. Just the thought of it was so upsetting, so *wrong* that he almost felt faint. Instead he said, "I don't know. What about you, though? Are you okay?"

She looked down at her hands. Then she opened her palm and shook a set of car keys.

"What are those?" Brooks asked.

"The keys to Lauren's Jeep. She's letting me borrow it tonight."

Brooks checked his watch. It was almost eleven. Where was Faith going at that hour? "What for?"

Faith looked around. They were still alone. "KC," she answered simply. "She's meeting a drug dealer in Walker Park at midnight. I have to stop her."

Everything else faded away. The sound of dishes in the kitchen, the murmur of the crowd, even the memory of glowing Melissa talking to his mom. "I want to go with you," Brooks heard himself say.

"You can't. You have to stay with Melissa."

Brooks reached out and grabbed Faith's arm. For some reason he had to go with her. If he was going to marry Melissa, he had to do something heroic. He had to feel like that white knight who could still stay on top of his horse. "I'm not supposed to see Melissa until tomorrow. Besides, I can't let you go to Walker Park alone."

"Brooks," Faith objected. "This is crazy. Leave this to me. It's insane for you to get involved!"

Brooks was already leading her toward the door. "Look, after tomorrow I may not be able to do insane things, or even help my friends. So please let me go with you."

Faith turned and looked right at him. "Brooks, you don't mean that, do you?"

"What?"

"About how getting married will end doing wild things and being with your friends. You don't really think that, do you?"

Brooks wasn't sure what he thought. He just knew that he had to move, to do, to save something or someone. To save himself. "I don't know any more," he told her. "I just know that KC is in trouble and I have to help."

Faith hesitated, but not for long. She took his hand. "I wouldn't let you do this if it wasn't so important," she said.

"Oh, it's important," he echoed. The coldness and queasiness he'd felt earlier were melting away. He felt more like himself. "It's important to KC," he said. "And it's important to me."

Twelve

"**A**re we on the right road, Winnie?"

"I don't know, Josh."

"Are we in the right state? The right country?"

"Josh, just keep the light on in the car, okay? And quit asking these funny questions. All I can tell is that we're on the right planet. No doubt about that at all. This is planet Earth."

"I think we should have rented a spaceship instead of borrowing Mikoto's car."

"Knowing Mikoto, this probably is a space-ship."

Josh didn't laugh at her lame joke. Instead,

more cars went by, more lights, more off-ramp signs, and more endless black sky. They were completely lost, and Winnie was starting to wish they'd never started out.

"Do you have any idea how much farther this shop is?" she asked.

"You want an honest answer?" Josh tossed back.

"No."

Josh nodded and adjusted the mirror. "Good."

They'd been tired when they left the country club. The wedding rehearsal and all the excitement and the anticipation had drained them. But they had to make this trip in just one night, then drive back immediately. Joe Tyler, the man who sold the crampons, had promised to open extra early in the morning just for them. So Winnie and Josh had agreed to share the driving, but with a turn each at the wheel they'd already caught the other drifting and swaying.

Winnie had made Josh pull over at a rest stop once so that she could give him what she called an "arresting and stimulating foot rub," but one that Josh claimed was "ouchy and terrible," and only designed to make him ache, not keep him awake. He preferred to put coins in the vending machine and drink a few "buzz your brain" sodas to keep him alert. After all, that's what he did when he pulled his famous all-nighters. And he reminded Winnie that she was hyperqueen of the U of S campus. If they couldn't make this trip in record time, then who could?

Turning up the radio to the loudest, most obnoxious station on the dial, they hit the road again. Josh was convinced that the two hours more of driving would pass quickly now that he and Winnie were recharged.

"Do you want me to look at the map?" Josh blurted.

Winnie frowned. She knew Josh had the male/logic/computer notion that she didn't understand maps. It made her furious, partly because she knew it wasn't true, and partly because it was so sexist. Unfortunately, right now she was so tired that she was having a hard time with the map. In fact, spread out on the car seat, and with the streetlights going by overhead and Josh only intermittently turning on the interior light, she couldn't really tell if she even had it right side up.

"I'll do it," she assured him.

"So where are we, Winnie?"

"We're somewhere close," Winnie said, wishing she hadn't said that.

"Close to what?"

"Close to the place."

"What place?"

"The place where we are."

Josh looked at her. A look of puzzlement momentarily penetrated his fatigue. "Huh?"

"Look," Winnie faked. She pushed the map at him. "You can see where we are."

"I can't see, Winnie, I'm driving."

"Well, do you want me to drive?"

"It's my turn to drive. It's my turn until we get there, then it's your turn after that."

"Well, we haven't gotten there yet."

"I know."

"And we won't get there until we're there."

"I know. But where are we on the map?"

"We're not there yet," Winnie said with absolute certainty. Then she folded her arms and refused to say anything more.

Josh sighed. "Okay, I'll pull over."

He slowed the car to a stop. Winnie was so tired that she couldn't even bring her body to take advantage of the situation. She just sat there like a lump without stretching, bending, or getting out to do sit-ups as she normally would.

Josh snapped on the interior light. They both groaned and Winnie covered her eyes.

"Are you okay?" Josh asked.

"No."

"Well, once I figure out where we are, we'll be fine."

"Humph. There's no need to act superior. Just because you're a guy doesn't mean you read maps better than I do. If I weren't so tired, we'd be there by now."

"Winnie, I'm not being sexist. And I can't concentrate with you yelling at me."

"You look so tired I'm not sure that you can concentrate *without* me yelling at you," Winnie insisted. "I'm just trying to help."

Josh glared at her. "Well, it doesn't help me." He picked up the map and rattled it and then held it up as if it were a screen that could block her out.

She reached over and punched at it.

"Winnie!"

Winnie could feel herself start to cry. She'd give anything right now to just find a nice warm bed and curl up and sleep, but that wasn't going to happen. Instead they were having this stupid fight because they'd bitten off more then they could chew and because it was the same old story—Josh was preoccupied, uncommunicative, remote, and hands-off; she was weird, flaky, disorganized, and impulsive.

"Look," Josh insisted, "you're not making this any easier."

"Would I make it easier if I told you the map was upside down?"

Josh looked at her, then looked back at the map. "How do you know that?"

"Because I gave it to you upside down. I didn't figure it out until you turned on the inside light."

"Great."

Winnie looked at Josh and suddenly began to smile.

He looked back at her and smiled, too. Then he began to laugh.

"Don't laugh," she teased. "Unless you're laughing at yourself."

Josh stuck one hand across the seat and tickled her.

"Josh!" Now Winnie began to laugh and tried to tickle him back.

"We're nuts," Josh admitted.

"That must be why we're together," agreed Winnie.

He lifted his arm, then pulled her in.

She scooted closer. "Do you know that I love you?" she asked, suddenly so full of love that she wanted to scream it to the passing cars.

He grinned. "Do you?"

"Yes, I do." She leaned her head on his shoulder. "You stood by me when you caught me being a flirty bozo with Matthew Callender. You've always stood by me. You even like my clothes."

He waved his hand in a fifty-fifty gesture.

"You mean you don't like my clothes?" she questioned.

He nudged her. "I like *you* in your clothes."

"That'll do," she said.

They started driving again after looking at the map. Soon Winnie knew from the signs that they had made it to Nevada, although she sensed that they were headed in the wrong direction.

"You know, I'm a lucky guy," Josh said. He cocked his head. "You didn't blow a fuse when I did a major computer-nerd session instead of making it to Brooks and Melissa's party on time. And you're funny and smart and sexy and a lot more."

"Really?"

"I'll say." He squeezed her arm. "How about pulling off the road and finding a place to stay? I'm beat. Besides, if we stop, we can show how much we love each other instead of just making speeches about it."

They drove down the nearest off-ramp, then on a desert road for a few miles. Soon a place that looked like a combo casino/motel came into view. A pink neon sign blinked DRIVE IN something. The front-door light was still lit up.

Josh pulled into the parking lot. He turned to Winnie and touched her face. "I could never feel lost with you," he said, leaning in to kiss her mouth.

Winnie embraced him. There were no more quips or comebacks. It was just she and Josh and a night full of pure love.

Cold, wet, weary.

KC was all of those things. She sat on a bench near the entrance to Walker Park and shivered in her mother's old rain poncho. Her hair was a mass of damp strings, her hands clammy. Her neck ached, her mouth tasted funny. A voice in the back of her head kept asking what she was doing here in the dead of night—but she stayed. She had to. Marielle expected her to be here, and right now Marielle was the only person she could count on. Every one of her other so-called friends couldn't be trusted.

Lately KC had spent a lot of time rehearsing what she would tell Faith and Winnie and Kimberly and Lauren if she had the chance. She'd tell them how she really felt about Peter going away, how one part of her was thrilled for his incredible opportunity to study overseas, and another part of her felt angry, jealous, and left behind. She'd tell them how her father was really doing, how he looked weaker and thinner every time she saw him. She'd tell them about how hard school had become, and how nothing seemed real anymore.

But who cares? KC almost shouted. Who cares?

She could be strong on her own. She could do daring things. And Marielle would do them with her. Marielle would never desert her the way Peter and her friends and her father had.

The wind came up and some dead leaves on the ground stirred. KC bit her lip and wrapped her arms around herself. That's when she heard a sound behind her. She turned, expecting to see Marielle, but it was Jed. He had appeared out of nowhere. KC had the funny feeling that he had been watching her for some time.

"Hi," she said first.

Jed was wearing a long green army coat this time, which made him look even taller. A red bandanna was tied around his neck, and a pair of black motorcycle boots covered his feet. He didn't say hello to KC, but instead pushed back his long, dark hair, and then made a circle around her, almost like an animal sniffing its prey.

"Are you alone?" he finally asked.

"Well, Marielle is going to meet us here," KC said. She checked her watch. "She's just a little late."

"So it's just you and me." Jed suddenly smiled and then sat down on the bench, stretching his long legs out and setting the heels of his boots down with a thud. "Now, that's kind of interesting, isn't it?" he suggested.

"Yeah, I guess," KC answered. She looked into the dark, praying for Marielle to appear. Her stomach had started to clench. She hadn't taken any pills in hours and her head ached.

"I brought your stuff," Jed bragged, his eyes welded to KC's as if they were powered by lasers. They were so intense that it dawned on KC that he was totally high.

Jed scooted closer to her on the bench and drummed on his thigh in triple time. Then he placed one foot over hers, as if he were trapping her. "You look cold. You know, I can give you whatever you need."

KC swallowed.

"You're so pretty," Jed continued. He stretched out his long arm and it moved to encircle her like a snake.

KC could smell Jed's dirty hair, and she guessed that he hadn't changed his clothes in days. But the worst thing was that even though everything about him was repulsive, Jed didn't seem to know it. He just kept those eyes locked on her while all the while his face was coming closer.

"Uh, stop," KC finally said, in a desperate move to slow him down.

"Stop what, college girl?"

"Um, stop and let's do the deal. Okay?"

Jed nodded. "Did Marielle give you the money?"

"Um, no." KC began to panic. Where was Marielle? Of all times for Marielle to desert her. It wasn't possible! "She'll be here any minute."

"I sure hope so, 'cause it's getting late. And you know we can't do any deal without money," Jed said, a menacing tone now appearing in his voice for the very first time. "Unless you got something else I might want."

The last words made KC want to vomit. It suddenly struck her. Marielle wasn't going to show. For some reason she'd let KC go to the park and then left her there to fend for herself. Marielle wasn't going to turn up if KC waited all night.

KC tried to remember if she had any money of her own on her. She knew that Jed would never let her off unless she paid him—one way or another.

"I have to hurry," she blurted out, hoping it would somehow throw him off track. She started to get up.

Jed reached out, angrily grabbed her by the waist, and shoved her back down on the bench. "Just relax," he warned. "I was just kidding when I said it was getting late. We've got lots of time."

"No, we don't. Somebody could come. The police might be around."

Jed laughed. "Are you kidding? The cops never bother with this part of the park." He leaned into KC, then put one hand on her shoulder while the other crawled up her leg. "Believe me, we're the only ones here."

KC froze.

"Don't you want to make a deal?" Jed questioned.

KC was suddenly in tears. All she wanted to do was get away, to be back in her dorm room or at the sorority. But Jed was pressing down on her, pinning her arms and trying to kiss her. The smell of his greasy hair filled her nostrils. His puffy wet lips were smearing themselves across her face. She fought back, using every ounce of strength she had, but Jed was incredibly strong, and he obviously wasn't afraid to hurt her.

"C'mon, college girl," he threatened, "you're not getting the pills for free."

KC tried to scream, but the next thing she knew Jed was sticking his hand over her mouth. Then she felt his hand on her blouse. She kicked at his shin.

Jed screamed and momentarily let go. KC shoved him as hard as she could and tried to get away. But his hand reached out like a claw and squeezed at her arm with animal fury. "You little—"

"Stop. Help!"

"Kayyyyy Ceeeee!" someone screamed back to her in the dark.

"We're coming!"

KC couldn't believe the voices were real. It had to be her imagination. But the next thing she knew, Jed was being twirled around on his feet like a spinning top. She looked up and saw a fist angrily land right between his eyes.

"Leave her alone!" she heard a guy shout.

KC wept as she saw that it was Brooks.

There was another blow, this one delivered to Jed's stomach. When Jed tried to hit back, hands were clawing at his eyes and neck. They belonged to Faith, who was punching and pounding at him with just as much fury as Brooks.

With blood pouring out of his nose, Jed turned around and began to run. Brooks was going after him, but Faith grabbed his arm. "Let him go, Brooks."

"I don't want to let him go. If I get my hands on him again, I'll—"

"KC needs us. We've got to get her out of here."

That made Brooks stop, although his face was flushed, his eyes were on fire, his hands were shaking at his sides. KC had never seen him like this.

Faith rushed to KC and put her arms around her. "Are you all right? My God, KC, you could have been hurt."

"I know. I know." Tears began pouring from KC's eyes. Sobs exploded in her throat. Her whole body trembled as if all her loneliness and fear was suddenly bursting out.

Faith and Brooks patted and hugged her. Then they propped her up between them and led her out of the park.

Thirteen

"Is KC going to be all right?"

"I think so."

Brooks stayed in the hall until Faith shut the door of KC's dorm room and turned to look up at him.

"Courtney will stay the night with her," Faith said. "I can't believe that Courtney came over here as soon as I called. She was sound asleep."

"I don't think I'll sleep at all tonight." Brooks sighed. They began walking down the hall.

"Me either," Faith agreed.

Brooks found himself tightening his fists simply thinking about Jed and his attack on KC. His knuckles still hurt from where he'd made contact with Jed's face. He wondered if people at the wedding would notice that his hands were bruised and swollen.

They walked out of Langston House, then lingered on the porch steps. Faith, too, still seemed upset.

"I don't want to go back to my dorm," Brooks said.

"How about going for a walk, then?" Faith asked.

Brooks didn't know what he wanted. Part of him wanted the night to go on forever. He might even have gone back to the park to have another round with Jed if it meant that the sun might not rise. He was a knight after all, he told himself. Even though his hands stung and his head pounded, he had proved himself. So why did another part of him want morning to come sooner rather than later?

"A walk sounds good."

In silence they began to stroll across the green. The dorm area was deserted. Brooks had the strangest urge to take Faith's hand, the way he'd done on a thousand walks home after seventh period in high school. Instead he stuffed his sore hands in his pockets and tried to clear his brain.

"Thanks for coming with me," Faith said, after a while. "KC needed you. And so did I."

"Really?" he murmured, amazed at how much Faith's words meant to him.

Faith nodded. "Of course. You were really brave."

Brooks almost stumbled. "So were you."

"Thanks." Faith kicked at the damp grass and stole a glance at Brooks. "What are you thinking?"

Brooks stopped walking and pulled Faith down onto the ground. Sitting so close to her, he felt just the opposite of brave. Even after his triumph in battle he felt like a terrified wimp who would run away if someone said boo.

He took a deep, painful breath. The expression on Faith's face was so open, so familiar. And yet he hadn't seen it since they'd arrived at the U of S. "How can you be sure about something?" he suddenly heard himself ask.

"What are you talking about?"

Brooks stared down at his hands.

"Is this about KC?" Faith asked. "Brooks?" She leaned over to look at him.

This time he couldn't look back at her. He was afraid of what he might feel.

"What is it?" Faith repeated. "Tell me."

Instead of answering, he asked another question. "How do you know when you really love someone?"

"I don't know," Faith responded, as if she were searching to figure it out. "I guess you just . . . know."

He hesitated. "And what if you think you know, and then you're not sure. Do you just jump in, like we did with that guy in the park? Do you just fight your feelings until you punch them so hard that you finally win?"

Faith was really staring at him now. She knelt on the grass in front of him so that she could look right in his face.

It was impossible for him not to meet her eyes now.

"What feelings are you talking about?" she wanted to know.

"Lots of feelings," he blurted. "Feelings that I don't love Melissa as much as I should. Feelings that I'm making some terrible mistake."

Faith looked stunned.

"Feelings for you," he added in a whisper.

Faith tugged at the end of the scarf she was wearing inside her suede jacket. "Me?"

"You." He'd said it again. Maybe a bolt of lightning would come down and strike him dead, but it couldn't be any worse than the way he already felt.

Faith suddenly stood up. "You want to go over to the Beanery and get some coffee?" she asked.

This reminded Brooks of when he'd first started taking Faith out in high school: the missed meanings; awkward pauses; not knowing what to say; trying to guess the whole time what she was thinking and how she was reacting. "Don't worry," he said. "I'm not going to do anything about it."

"About what?"

He shook his head. "About my feelings for you. About my feelings that I'm about to make some terrible mistake."

Faith stepped back, as if she'd just been thrown a huge mental bomb that she needed to absorb. "Come on, let's walk and get some coffee. I think we need to talk."

They quickly crossed the campus and University Avenue, the cold no longer biting so hard, the night stars twinkling overhead. When they opened the door to the Beanery, Brooks almost fell over in shock. It was just the way it always was on a late Saturday night—crowded, busy, and loud. No one seemed to have any idea that he and Faith had just saved KC. And no one knew that Melissa was sleeping at the Springfield Country Club, waiting to be married tomorrow. Why should they? Their world wasn't about to change—just his.

He and Faith ordered espressos, then found a table to themselves. There was a guitar player on the mini bandstand and a fire in the fireplace at the end of the room. Brooks wanted to stop time and stay there forever.

But Faith had that no-avoiding-reality glare. "Do you still want to marry Melissa?" she asked.

"It was my idea," was his only answer.

"That's not what I asked," she pressed. "Do you still love her?"

Brooks almost spilled his coffee, his bruised hand was shaking so hard. "I don't know anymore," he finally admitted. Just saying it was like wrenching something from his gut. He was on the verge of tears.

"You were eloping a week ago. You loved her then. Don't you think you should know if you still do before you marry her?" Faith asked.

"Of course I should know," he blurted, no

longer able to keep anything back. "But everything's happening so fast, I haven't had time to think. Suddenly all my family is here and there are all these presents and plans. I can't stop it now!"

"When do you want to stop it?" Faith countered. "In the divorce court a year from now?"

Her directness was like a fist in his stomach. "That's not the point. Melissa is counting on me. Everyone is counting on me. I can't let Melissa down!"

Faith looked outraged. "You don't think you'll be letting her down if you marry her even though you're not really sure?"

"What is sure!" he almost yelled. "Who is ever sure? Of anything?"

Faith pushed back her chair and started out of the Beanery.

Brooks hurried to follow her, the images in his head becoming more confused. He thought of Melissa's face, but then he flashed on himself and Faith on prom night senior year.

Outside, Brooks felt a wave of dizziness. He thought he might pass out.

Faith stopped and turned back to face him. He grabbed her shoulders almost before he realized it.

"Brooks," she warned.

"I'm sorry," he said in a crazy voice. "I won't say stuff like this anymore. I won't even think it."

"Brooks, you can't tell yourself what to think," she insisted. "Or what to feel."

That was when something broke through. He could no longer stop himself. He reached for her, pressed his cheek against her blond hair. He thought she would push him away, but then he noticed that she was crying. She touched the back of his head.

"It'll be okay, Brooks. Be brave. Be honest. That's what you have to do."

And that was when he did it. Brooks closed his eyes and kissed her, his head reeling as his lips met hers. It was a long kiss that made him dizzy and happy and sad all at the same time.

Faith didn't pull back until the kiss was over. Then she touched his face with incredible gentleness. "Oh, Brooks," was all she could say.

"I know," he heaved as they began to walk back to the dorms. "That was a kiss for old times' sake. I'm still getting married tomorrow. Maybe I'm not the sane predictable guy everybody thought I was, but I'll be there for Melissa. I'll marry her."

Faith walked silently with him until they reached Coleridge Hall.

"Be true to yourself," she said.

He nodded and started to walk toward his dorm. He made himself promise he wouldn't look back.

Fourteen

Morning came. Birds chirped. Sunlight warmed the ground. Melissa opened her eyes. It took a moment for her to adjust to the strange room. When she turned over and saw the fancy towels in the bathroom, it all came back. You're staying at a room in the Springfield Country Club, she thought. This is where you'll get ready. In a few hours your wedding will begin!

She got up and out of habit did the same exercises she did before a track meet. After that she called Kimberly and Lauren. They were just about to leave and would be there in a few minutes. Faith had called and would be late because she'd been up all night with friends. Finally Melissa talked to her mom. She planned to arrive within the hour.

That left only one person to call—Brooks.

Melissa dialed the number of his dorm. His roommate, Barney, answered their hall phone. It turned out that Brooks had gone out for a jog around campus. Barney was sure he'd call later, but Brooks and Melissa had agreed that they wouldn't see each other before the ceremony— that would be bad luck.

After Melissa took a shower, she slipped on her everyday clothes and then answered the door when she heard a knock. Lauren and Kimberly had arrived, each holding a breakfast tray provided by the country club. Croissants, coffee, and orange juice were heaped on plates. "Wow," Melissa said.

"Not bad, huh?" Lauren agreed. She was wearing a jogging suit, but in her other hand carried her bridesmaid dress on a hanger. "You might get used to staying here."

Melissa grinned. "We're spending our honeymoon night at the club."

Kimberly gestured down the hall. "The staff is already getting ready for the wedding."

Melissa looked in the direction Kimberely was pointing. Sure enough, the club's staff, all in kelly-green jackets, were arranging flowers in the foyer, while others were wheeling carts of china and silver into the main hall. "I can't believe this," Melissa finally said.

"We can't either," said Lauren. "You're my first friend to get married."

The girls went into the room and shut the door. They began to eat and talk. Kimberly almost immediately began fiddling with Melissa's hair. "You are going to look beautiful," she said. "I can't wait to get started."

"Should I bring out your dress?" Lauren asked. She had stood up and was walking over to the closet. "I think you should try it on just so we can have another look."

"Okay."

Lauren came back with the huge box that held the dress. She put it on the bed and then carefully unpacked it. The silk and satin foil rustled as it unfolded in Lauren's arms. When it was completely revealed, Melissa took a sudden sharp breath. "I can't believe I'm really supposed to wear that," she admitted. "It's exquisite."

"I could wear it, but then Brooks might

marry the wrong person," Lauren joked as she unzipped the dress so Melissa could step into it.

The dress flowed over Melissa's body like a dream.

"God!" Lauren said.

"Wow!" Kimberly added.

Both girls stared at her, and Melissa knew why. She had never, ever looked more radiant.

"You look like a princess," Kimberly said.

"Yeah. Princess Di would die if she saw you."

They all laughed, and then Kimberly and Lauren tended to Melissa like the mice in *Cinderella*. "It's so gorgeous," Lauren said. She tucked and smoothed the satin and lace. "It fits perfectly."

Melissa thought about what the dress meant to her. She thought of all the time she and Brooks had spent together: the rough spots and the love. She remembered how close they'd come to eloping. Now things were turning out better than she'd ever imagined.

There was another knock at the door. "Hello . . ." a voice called. Kimberly ran to open the door and Melissa turned around to see her mother. Mrs. McDormand's face was a mixture of joy, surprise, and sadness. Melissa immediately ran over to hug her. "Is this my baby?" her mom said, beginning to cry.

Kimberly laughed. "She's certainly turned into a beautiful baby."

Melissa's mother nodded. Both she and Melissa had tears now. "Honey, maybe you should take the dress off before it gets totally wrinkled," Mrs. McDormand suggested. "It'd be a shame it it didn't look crisp for the ceremony."

"She's right," Kimberly agreed, "because I'm about to get down to business." She reached down and pulled out her cosmetic case. Inside were tons of mascaras, lipsticks, powders, blushes, eyeliners . . . everything.

So with the help of her mom and Lauren, Melissa took the dress off, then Kimberly whisked her over to the dressing table and began to work on her hair and makeup.

"People are beginning to arrive," Mrs. McDormand told the girls. "Aunt Betty and Uncle Max are here. Your cousins Addie and Tom came, too. This is the first wedding they've ever attended."

"I bet they'll remember it for a long time," Lauren predicted.

She was going through the closet, gathering up Melissa's slip, garter, stockings, and everything else that would go on *under* the wedding dress. Melissa sat patiently while Kimberly worked on her foundation. She began wondering about the rest of the wedding party. "Has anyone heard from Winnie and Josh?" she asked.

Kimberly shook her head. "I'd thought they'd call by now."

"Who knows what those two are doing," Lauren speculated. "But you can be sure that they'll be around for ceremony."

"And what about Brooks?" Kimberly mumbled, a lip pencil in her mouth.

Melissa smiled, thinking about Brooks. "I bet he went out with the guys last night."

"Stag party . . . disgusting," Lauren commented, but without sounding too critical.

"Boys will be boys," Kimberly suggested.

"Actually, I called Brooks's dorm and Barney said he went jogging this morning."

"You're kidding. That sounds like something you'd do, Mel."

Melissa smiled. Kimberly began to do her eye makeup. "I guess Melissa is already having an influence," she joked.

"I sure hope so," Melissa answered. Then she just sat back and enjoyed being pampered and powdered while she thought about her fiancé.

* * *

Two hours later Kimberly and Lauren were outfitted in their bridesmaid dresses and peeking outside the door of Melissa's room.

"Wow, it's happening," Kimberly realized. She looked down the hallway and into the foyer adjacent to the main room. Where before busboys and other country-club staff had been, now milled people outfitted in suits, dresses, and jackets. Both young and old seemed to be enjoying this time before the wedding ceremony.

Lauren sniffed at one of the many, many bouquets that were just inside the doorway of Melissa's room. "This is going to be great," she commented. "Have you ever seen so many flowers?"

"The ideal big wedding."

"Yes, and the perfect blending of Brooks's and Melissa's family."

"They seem to be getting along great," Kimberly remarked. She couldn't really tell where Brooks's family started and Melissa's family left off, although from everything that Melissa had told her, it seemed like she should be able to tell. The Baldwins and McDormands

178 • **Linda A. Cooney**

were supposed to be as different as families could be, but then Melissa wasn't known to be the most objective observer.

Kimberly also spotted some of Brooks's old friends from high school, as well as new ones from college. There were people from student government, the climbing club, soccer, the honors society—Kimberly couldn't believe how many people Brooks knew. It was great, too, that all of them thought enough of Brooks to come to his wedding. It gave Kimberly hope. Here was someone of the opposite sex who was really a good guy, a person that both men and women respected. If Melissa could find a guy like that, why couldn't she?

Lauren nudged Kimberly. "Look, there're some of the band members."

Kimberly smiled. "Yeah, I think Melissa's dad is making them rehearse his version of 'It Had to Be You' so he can sing to Melissa after the ceremony."

"I'd die a thousand deaths."

"I think it's sweet," Kimberly said. Melissa's dad being sentimental fit in with the mellow mood she was beginning to get into. She wasn't even steaming in quite the same way she had been over Derek.

Suddenly a catering person whisked by carrying a tray of smoked salmon. Lauren shook her head in amazement. "What about the food? Can you believe it? I mean, I've never seen so many elegant catered dishes in my life. They have everything from Chinese to Cajun to Nouvelle California. And that's just the hors d'oeuvres."

"Excuse me, please."

Both girls looked to the left and saw another country-club employee standing there holding two gigantic boxes wrapped in bows and shiny paper. He nodded as two guests let him by. "More presents," Kimberly acknowledged. "There's a whole mountain of them in the reception room already."

Lauren laughed. "Melissa's going to have a lot of thank-you notes to write."

Kimberly tried standing on her tiptoes to get the best look over the heads of the crowd. She hoped to catch a glimpse of Brooks. It would be a moral booster to spot a really handsome, really *nice* guy. Besides, she was getting more and more curious. "You haven't seen Brooks yet," she said casually.

"No, of course not. We're not supposed to see him until that final march up the aisle."

"Oh Lauren, you're such a killjoy," Kimberly teased. She giggled. "Bet he's nervous."

Lauren folded her arms. "I don't know why. There're only about five hundred guests here."

"Yeah, and probably half of them from out of town."

Kimberly looked back over her shoulder into the room. She was really proud of the way Melissa was handling herself. There was a lot of pressure, but considering this was the girl who used to climb the walls before a track meet, her reaction to her impending wedding was reason to celebrate.

"Melissa is incredibly together," Kimberly said. "I hope that doesn't mean Brooks is falling apart. You know what they say about couples taking on each other's characteristics."

"I doubt it," Lauren said. "I just hope Winnie and Josh show up soon. Can't you picture Winnie rushing up to the altar at the last minute?"

"Yeah. Melissa might think she's in a track meet and Winnie is gaining on her."

"Or Brooks might mistake her for that one last girl throwing herself at his feet."

"Oh, we're cruel." Kimberly laughed. "Too cruel."

Lauren went back to help Melissa while Kimberly continued to peek out the door. She loved spying on people. The excitement in the air was palpable and it was fun to watch everyone interacting.

Suddenly Kimberly's mood shifted. "Derek!" she whispered.

She slipped out of the room, even though it really was against the rules to let any of the wedding party be seen before the ceremony, but heck, Winnie and Josh hadn't shown up, and Kimberly hungered to talk to Derek, to finally pin him down and get the facts.

She cornered him just as he was about to walk into the main hall.

"I'm glad to catch you before things get started," Kimberly said.

"Hi," Derek said, in a tightly controlled voice. He was dressed in the same black formal wear as the rest of the men in the wedding party. "I was expecting to see you here."

"Good," Kimberly answered, "because I've *really* been wanting to talk to you."

"No fooling?"

"No fooling," Kimberly mimicked. "Follow me." She maneuvered between the crowd until they were off in a corner near the glass doors that separated the foyer from the swimming-pool area.

Derek looked puzzled. No doubt he had detected a hint of hostility and frustration in Kimberly's voice. He took a step back. "Is there a problem?"

"Yes," Kimberly admitted. "And I think the problem is you."

"Me?"

"Yes, you, Derek. I don't appreciate being bombarded with notes, and invitations, and corny messages every time I turn around. I thought we'd agreed to respect each other, to be friends."

"We did," Derek insisted.

"So why all the notes, then?"

"Notes?" Derek looked completely flummoxed. He stared at Kimberly as if she were slightly deranged.

"Look," she stormed, "do I have to bring you fingerprints? You know what I'm talking about."

"No, I don't."

"Yes, you do."

Derek arched an eyebrow and then showed the slightest bemused smile. "You'll have to tell me, Kimberly."

"Okay, I will, since you're being a jerk about it. The notes."

Derek looked as puzzled as ever. "The notes . . ." he repeated.

"That you've been leaving me."

"That I've been leaving you."

"Yes."

"Where?"

"You know where. Everywhere. And it's not just notes. It's flowers, too. And—"

"Wait a minute. Wait a minute, Please," Derek interrupted. "I'm not leaving you anything. It's not me."

"What do you mean it's not you? Of course it's you. Who else would do such a thing?"

"I don't know." Derek smiled. "I guess maybe some crazy guy out there thinks you're an interesting person. You might have figured it out if you weren't paranoid."

"Paranoid!" Kimberly barked.

"Yes, I think it's a little paranoid that you suspect me of doing something that I obviously haven't done."

Kimberly stared, dumbfounded. "You mean you did . . . did . . . didn't," she finally stammered out.

"No, I didn't, Kimberly. Actually, you really

aren't on my mind every thinking, waking moment."

"Well, I don't expect you to say that I am."

"But obviously there *is* some poor guy out there who has a thing for you. I suggest you find out who he is so you can talk to him and show him the error of his ways."

"Very funny, Derek."

"I don't know, Kimberly, you just seem to bring out the comedian in me."

"Ooooooohhhhhhh!"

"Ta-ta." Derek gave a casual wave and then sauntered off, looking more confident than ever.

Kimberly was angry, more at herself than at Derek. She had spoken to him when there was no need to. But if Derek wasn't leaving her notes, who was? Without coming up with a likely candidate, she headed back toward Melissa's room.

"Faith, you look worried," Lauren whispered.

Faith nodded. She was quickly adjusting her dress, her heels, and her makeup. Having arrived only ten minutes earlier, she had apologized to Melissa for oversleeping, but Lauren noticed that her ex-roommate looked tired and upset.

Faith put down her lipstick and faced her friend. "I am a little worried," she admitted.

"About Winnie and Josh not being here yet?" Lauren queried.

"Yes, sure. I mean it is getting late, although I'm one to talk."

"Did you get enough sleep last night?"

"Not really." Faith hesitated, then finally spoke up. "I was up talking to KC."

Lauren nodded. That explained it. They were all worried about KC. She was going through a terrible time. She'd become almost like a stranger. It made Lauren sad even to think about it. "Maybe I should go out and look for Winnie," she suggested.

"I bet she's in the parking lot," Faith said. "And I'm predicting she's all dressed and she's out there trying to balance champagne glasses or something on her nose."

Lauren giggled. "I can just see her." Still, she was worried. "I have to go look around," she said in the next breath. "I'll die if she's not in the wedding. I know she will, too."

"Okay, see you in a little bit."

"If Melissa asks . . ."

"I'll just tell her you got flaky," Faith joked. "Now go. Hurry."

Lauren did just that, but not before stopping by the closet and finding her raincoat. She threw it on over her bridesmaid dress so no one out in the main hall would be any the wiser, then she got going.

There were dozens and dozens of faces to be seen—none of them Winnie's—all belonging to people apparently having a wonderful time. Lauren recognized some of Melissa's brothers and sisters; Brooks's grandma; an uncle of Melissa's who'd come all the way from Missouri.

"Excuse me. I'm sorry. So sorry," Lauren said as she brushed past one person after another. "Could I get by? Excuse me."

She was a regular "Excuse me" machine. No one was giving her dirty looks yet. The mood was too joyous, but weaving through another group of guests, Lauren suddenly found herself in front of a stern and implacable face.

"Hello, Lauren."

Lauren stopped. She felt herself beginning to get hot. The face belonged to Dash. But for once he wasn't wearing army pants, a bandanna, or a sleeveless T-shirt. Instead he wore a soft, navy-blue blazer, crisp beige pants, and a pink cotton shirt that caught the color and texture of his olive skin. She'd almost never seen him look so handsome. "Hi," she said, hoping that she wasn't letting on that he looked more than spectacular.

"Isn't it almost time to start?" Dash asked.

"Yeah."

"I suppose I should go and sit down."

Lauren noted the indecisiveness of that comment. It didn't sound like the old Dash she knew and, unfortunately, once loved. This sounded like a Dash who just might not be so sure of himself. "How do you like weddings?" she asked quickly while putting her hands in her raincoat pockets without thinking.

"That's a weird question."

"Why?"

"I don't know. How do *you* like them?"

"I like them just fine when everybody shows up on time. That reminds me. Have you seen Winnie or Josh?"

"No."

"Great."

"Was I supposed to?"

Lauren shook her head. "They're both in the wedding party."

"And you're out looking for them."

"You have the instincts of a great reporter, Dash Ramirez," Lauren said, trying to lighten the mood with a joke.

"Not really," Dash parried. "A great editor maybe, but you, actually, are the great reporter."

"Flattery just might get you somewhere," Lauren said, but she didn't smile when she said it.

"Speaking of reporting," Dash went on, "you know when I talked to you the other day?"

"Yes."

"Well, I thought I might come by again and—"

"I'm living with Winnie now."

"You mean you replaced—"

"Melissa," they both said at the same time.

There was a moment of strained silence. Lauren knew she should be going, but for some weird reason she wanted to stay. She didn't have the faintest idea why. It was clear that she and Dash were destined to talk right past each other for the rest of their lives. Her mind accepted that, but her heart was still hoping for more.

"I really have to look for Winnie."

"I'll keep an eye out, too."

"Thanks. If you see her send her straight to Melissa's room," Lauren instructed. "It's right over there." She pointed in the opposite direction.

Dash nodded. "Okay. Nice talking to you."

"Nice talking to you, too."

Lauren turned around. She took a deep breath and then walked off, suppressing a desire to scream and cry and yell. She wanted to tell Dash that he was such a jerk—that they were both jerks for not being able to communicate anymore.

A tear rolled off her eyelid. Lauren brushed it aside. She shouldn't be reacting this way. It was all over with Dash. There was nothing she could do about that anymore.

"I just want to find Winnie," she muttered, even though deep down she knew that Winnie wasn't the person she was really looking for at all.

Fifteen

"**I**s that music?" Faith gasped.

Kimberly slipped a corsage onto her wrist and nodded. "The pianist just started. That means it's time for the ushers to seat everybody."

"But Winnie and Josh still haven't gotten here. Maybe we should wait for them."

"I don't think we can." Kimberly shrugged. "It's just a good thing Melissa's cousin is the maid of honor. We'll have to go ahead, even if we are short one bridesmaid."

After the way she and Brooks had kissed the night before, Faith hadn't been sure if Brooks was going to cancel the wedding or if he'd go ahead as planned. The fact that everything was in full swing, though, meant that Brooks had calmed down and wanted to make Melissa his bride. Faith propped open the door and looked out again. She didn't see anyone else in the wedding party. Lauren had gone to the bathroom. Melissa was with her parents. The guys were ushering guests.

"What about Brooks?" Faith was almost afraid to ask. "Do you know if he's here yet?"

Kimberly finally betrayed some anxiety of her own. "I don't know. Funny how even a nice guy like him isn't on time to his own wedding."

Faith didn't reply. Instead she grabbed her corsage and lunged into the hall. She'd spotted Barney, Brooks's roommate. A weightlifter, Barney bulged in his rented tux.

"Barney!" Faith cried.

Barney sped over to meet her.

"Has Brooks shown up yet?" she blurted.

Barney shook his head. "He said he wanted time to himself back at the dorm. I guess he's savoring his last minutes of freedom. I told that Harcourt guy that he would get here just before the ceremony."

"Oh." Faith tensed as more people passed

them and took their places in the hall.

"But Brooks still has to get into his tux," Barney explained. He tried to adjust his collar, which looked painfully tight. "It's hanging in one of the dressing rooms. I know it won't take him more than five minutes to get dressed, but this is pushing it pretty close. He'll be here, though."

Faith nodded. She remembered Brooks's last words to her. *I'll marry her,* he'd said. Brooks never went back on his word. "I know he will," she whispered. She shifted her body and watched the crowd. "It's just feeling like missing-persons day. Or late-persons day. First Winnie and Josh, now Brooks."

"There's still at least ten minutes," Barney muttered. "I'm sure everything will be fine."

Faith and Barney went silent as Canon Harcourt marched by. He backtracked when he saw them. "Where's the bride?" he asked cheerfully.

Faith and Barney looked at one another. "She's still with her mom and her cousin, in Room 112, I think," Faith replied.

Canon Harcourt nodded, as if that were the perfect place for Melissa to be. "I'll go get her," he said. He smiled at Faith. "You round up the bridesmaids." Then he looked at Barney. "And you tell Brooks to meet us out here in five minutes. It's almost time to start. He's probably getting dressed."

Barney nodded blankly. As soon as Harcourt left, he looked at Faith again.

"I'll go tell the pianist to add a few extra songs," Faith decided.

"Good idea."

Faith patted Barney's arm, then skirted into the hall. The smell of perfume and flowers almost knocked her over. Equally overwhelming was the sense of joyful anticipation. Women hugged and chattered. Men looked proud. Little kids stood in their best clothes.

With great subtlety Faith asked the pianist to pad the musical introduction. That done, she began to hurry out to gather the other bridesmaids and wait for Canon Harcourt.

But as she scampered up the aisle, a hand extended and reached out to her. At the same time Faith heard a tired but hopeful voice.

"Faith."

For a second Faith closed her eyes. "KC," she said almost in a whisper.

KC was in an aisle seat, about halfway back. She wore a simple knit dress that Faith recognized from high school. Her hair was freshly washed and combed. She still looked pale and tired, but for the first time in weeks Faith saw the old knockout KC beauty.

"Is it almost time?" KC asked.

Faith was suddenly happier to see KC than she could ever have been to see Josh and Winnie, or even Brooks. She knelt down and put her hand on KC's arm. "You came."

KC shrugged. "I was invited." She looked down.

"You know what I mean," Faith said.

"I know."

They looked into each other's eyes for a moment. "Did you get some sleep last night?" Faith asked in a whisper.

KC nodded and leaned forward so they could hear one another over the music. "Courtney stayed the whole night. She slept on my floor. Can you believe it? What a friend."

Faith nodded.

Tears filled KC's eyes. She looked away again, as if it was too much for her to stare into Faith's eyes. "You too," she finally said.

Faith took her hand.

"Thank you," KC whispered. "Thank you and Brooks for last night. I think it's the end between me and Marielle."

Faith didn't gloat or grin or judge. This time she just listened.

"I've been having a really hard time," KC admitted. "Maybe I can't save my dad, or bring Peter back, but I have to turn things around for myself." She looked down again. "No one's going to do it for me."

There was nothing more to say just then. And that was good, because at that exact moment Faith saw Winnie scurrying down the aisle. Winnie looked radiant, as if she could light up the sky with her own joy. She smiled warmly at KC, then grabbed Faith.

"Well, what are you waiting for, Faith?" Winnie said, grinning. She was wearing the regulation bridesmaid gear, but her earrings were teddy bears dotted with green and yellow sequins. "We're all outside and ready to go. Let's get this show on the road!"

Faith shot to her feet. *"Is Brooks here?"* she gasped.

"Of course he's here," Winnie answered, as if Faith were insane. They left KC and started out to the hall. Winnie was still grinning as if she'd just won the lottery. "Brooks is here. Josh is here. I guess the three of us were a little late, but I've always said that promptness is the sign of an unbalanced personality."

In spite of her memory of the previous night, Faith felt incredibly relieved.

Melissa had a delicious, wacky flash of her coach pumping his runners up for a big track meet. That was because she was standing on one side of Canon Harcourt, Brooks was on the other, and the rest of the wedding party were around all three of them as the minister gave last-minute instructions. Well, if this were like a big meet, she told herself, it was one she was going to win . . . forever and ever.

"Is everybody clear on everything?" Canon Harcourt asked.

The ushers nodded.

The bridesmaids grinned.

Melissa's cousin, her parents, and Brooks's all fell into a line.

"Sorry we were so late," Winnie blurted. "But we had an amazing, amazing adventure."

She was shushed by Lauren, who looked ultra-serious and proper.

Finally Melissa looked at her husband-to-be. No matter how much she'd savored her last night and morning as a single person, she was thrilled at the prospect of pledging her love to Brooks. Brooks was the one and only guy for her. There were no doubts in her mind anymore. Looking at him again, she was reminded of how handsome and loving and steady he was—even if he did look awfully pale.

She sidestepped Canon Harcourt and gave Brooks a hug.

He didn't respond.

She started to giggle. "Barney and Derek threatened to take you out last night and get you really drunk. That's what they did, didn't they?"

Brooks didn't answer.

Melissa looked at him one last time and felt the iciness of his skin. She giggled to herself as she thought about how much the guys had probably made Brooks drink, and how sick he'd probably gotten.

Suddenly they all heard the pianist play a very familiar piece.

"Yikes, the Wedding March," Winnie shrieked. She grinned back at Josh. "Here we go."

Canon Harcourt propped open the door to the hall. He smiled at Melissa, then at Brooks.

Melissa couldn't see Brooks anymore

because she'd taken her father's shaky arm and was beginning to walk in. As she slowly descended the aisle her dress billowed. Everyone stared and beamed at her. Tears of joy rolled down her face. She felt as if she were sailing on a pillow of sunshine, trusting happiness, and light.

She took her place at the altar. Her father, with tears in his eyes, bent down and kissed her tenderly on the cheek. Melissa hugged him and then gave Brooks her hand. They were standing side by side. Canon Harcourt was opening his book.

"We are gathered together today . . ."

Melissa glanced at Brooks, who was staring blankly at the minister. She suddenly wished that he hadn't gone out drinking with his buddies and then wondered why she was even thinking such a thing in the middle of her wedding.

The ceremony started to go by quickly. Canon Harcourt went on about love and some parable about renting rooms in a big apartment and each room being full of new challenges. But Melissa listened less and less, because more and more she was aware of Brooks's paleness. Beads of sweat had broken out all over his face. He was still holding her hand, but his palm was damp and limp.

"Brooks, do you take Melissa to be your lawful wedded wife? To have and to hold . . ."

The words were dreamlike. Melissa wasn't sure how they had gotten there so fast, but she was ready. She looked at Brooks. She wanted to smile, but her mouth was trembling. Instead, she squeezed his hand and waited for his answer.

"Uh . . ." was all he said.

"Brooks, do you take Melissa to be your lawful wedded wife? To have and to hold," the minister repeated.

Brooks was sweating heavily now. He let go of her hand and took a step away.

Melissa realized that something was wrong. The minister had closed the pages of the book.

"Brooks," she said quietly. "Brooks?"

"Brooks," the minister began, opening his book again. "Do you take Melissa to be your lawful wedded—"

"Uh . . ." Brooks stuttered. "Uh . . . I don't think I can go through with this," he said in a barely audible voice.

There was a quick gasp from Faith, then a collective one from the others in the wedding party.

People began to whisper. Melissa's mother came foward.

"What?" Melissa managed.

Brooks looked right at her. "I don't think we should do this," he choked. "I don't think *I* can do it. I can't marry you."

Melissa suddenly felt as if she were falling into a nightmare. Her heart tumbled in a mess of fear and confusion.

"Brooks, please!"

"I'm so sorry, Melissa. I'm so sorry. I just can't do this. It's all been a huge mistake. I'm not ready. It wouldn't be fair to you. I . . . I . . . I . . ."

Melissa turned away. All the faces she saw looked sorry, too. There was pain on Faith's face, tears in Lauren's eyes. She tried to take the first step, but then she felt sweat cover her own brow. A horrible feeling lurched up from the pit of her stomach. The room darkened and whirled.

"Melissa!" Brooks cried out.

That was the last thing Melissa heard before she fell to the ground and everything went black.

Sixteen

....

"Some party."

"Who said that?"

"That's an awful thing to say."

"Well, what are we supposed to say?"

"I don't know. Let's see if we can change our plane reservations and go home early."

Winnie watched another pair of out-of-town guests, looking betrayed and hurt, wander out of the Springfield Country Club. Only the wedding bouquets, the china and goblets and food weren't going anywhere. And neither was Winnie. She was one of the few people left who didn't feel droopy and dulled.

But she'd had to keep her explosive joy to herself while the others mourned the end of Melissa and Brooks.

She shared a piece of wedding cake with Josh. When they were sure that no one was looking, they kissed through the frosting and grinned at each other.

What few people remained milled around as if they were at a funeral. Lauren was still crying. Kimberly kept muttering. KC was pale and silent. Faith looked exhausted. Winnie clung to Josh, refusing to let go.

"Poor Brooks," Faith whispered. "Poor Melissa."

"He'll be okay," Winnie said, sidestepping a table to put her arm around Faith. "So will Melissa. In about a hundred thousand years."

Lauren marched over, too. "But how could he do this to her?"

"They're going to hate each other for life," Kimberly moaned. She stripped off her corsage and tossed it onto the floor. "I don't know if Melissa will ever get over this."

"How can she?" Lauren said glumly. "She was totally humiliated."

"Yeah, but if Brooks felt it was wrong," Faith protested.

"Then he should have called it off earlier," Kimberly said.

Faith took a breath. "I think Brooks *did* want to call it off before this. I think he was trying. He just didn't know how."

There was silence. The mood changed a little. Some sympathy for Brooks seemed to go around.

"He won't lose his friends," Josh said first, as tentative as Winnie about saying something positive.

"He's lost Melissa, and she was his *best* friend," Lauren reminded them. "Or she should have been."

"Poor Melissa," Kimberly repeated. "I hope this is the last wedding I'm invited to for a long time."

Winnie stifled a giggle. So did Josh.

Kimberly glared at them.

There was more silence. A busboy who was cleaning up dropped a glass and it rolled across the carpet. The hotel staff was moving in, starting to fold up chairs and take them away.

Winnie locked eyes with Josh again and she could no longer contain the bubbles of joy inside her. It wasn't her fault if terrible things happened to some people, while wonderful things happened to others. She smiled. Josh smiled, too. Then he kissed her, for so long their friends started to stare. When Winnie pulled back, she touched Josh's face and they both began to laugh.

"I'm glad you two find this so amusing," Kimberly said.

"Why are you laughing?" Lauren asked.

Faith frowned. "Winnie, what's going on?"

Winnie looked at Josh.

He looked at her.

"Shall we tell them?" she asked.

"It's not really a great time," he said.

"No time is perfect, I guess," Winnie countered, "although this is about as perfect a time as I've ever had."

Josh smiled at her again while the rest of them frowned as if she'd been the one to ruin the wedding.

"What?" Faith prompted.

"Um . . . Josh and I have an announcement," Winnie spoke up, in what for her was an untypically small voice.

They all stared at her—even Josh, as if he had no idea what she was going to say.

"Winnie, please don't make this any worse," Lauren said with a sigh. "I think we all understand what just happened here."

"Well, it was dreadful," Winnie admitted, "but there's always a brighter side."

"Oh, really?" said Kimberly.

Winnie perched on the table. "There is, Kimberly. Believe me. I know that I have kind of a screwy outlook on life, but trust me on this one."

Lauren shook her head. "Well, there's no question about them getting together and talking very soon. There's too much hurt."

"Just listen," Winnie advised. She smiled at Josh and was flooded with more happiness. "I mean, look at me. I've done stupid things in the past—like the time I met Josh at the toga party and, you know, kind of messed things up."

"Winnie," Kimberly interrupted, "what's your point?"

"Um, the point is that I have an announcement."

"You said that already." Kimberly sighed. "So make it."

Winnie blushed. Josh put his arm around her and she leaned against him. "Want me to tell them?" he asked.

Winnie shook her head. "Late last night . . .

Josh and me . . . we were driving along—"

"Lost," Josh filled in.

"Yeah, really lost," Winnie chattered. "So lost we were actually fighting about it. And then we stopped and realized it was dumb to fight."

"This is all I want to hear," moaned Lauren, "more depressing news about male/female relationships."

"But that's just the point, Lauren," Winnie interjected, her voice rising in pitch, "I mean, it's not *all* bad news. It really isn't."

"Prove it," Kimberly dared.

Winnie laughed. "Well, I will. So we were fighting about how to read the map and stuff, 'cause we had to find this place that sold crampons—you know we were buying them for Brooks and Melissa as a wedding present . . . for mountain climbing . . ."

Another groan went out from their friends.

Winnie flapped her hands. Josh kissed her cheek. "I know. I know. It's depressing. But believe me, it gets better, because pretty soon we both agreed we were totally lost and decided to take the next exit and found this place that was all lit up with neon signs even though it was really late at night."

"So what happened?" Faith asked impatiently.

"Well, it turned out to be this place that was kind of like an all-night convenience store of matrimony, you know, sort of like a 7-Eleven chapel of love," Winnie explained.

"Yeah," Josh admitted, "the place could sell you marriage licenses."

"What!" They now had Faith's full attention. The others were beginning to lean forward as well.

"Yeah, and that wasn't all. There was this little wedding chapel with black velvet paintings on the walls. I especially liked the one of Elvis."

"Elvis?" Lauren questioned.

"Yep." Winnie laughed. "Weird, huh. I loved it. Josh did, too. We both agreed that this was the weirdest, nerdiest, nuttiest wedding chapel combination convenience store that we'd ever seen. Of course we'd never seen one before."

KC looked at Winnie in disbelief. She took a step toward her old friend. "So tell us, Win, tell us," she said softly, speaking up for the first time.

"Well, we decided to buy a wedding license," Winnie explained.

"And then we decided to get married," Josh added quickly.

"What?" said all their friends at once.

"Yeah, that's right," Josh interrupted. He nestled closer to Winnie. "We ended up getting married in the Chapel d'Elvis."

There was a full thirty seconds of complete and utter silence. Faith folded her arms, looked at the ground, refolded her arms, and then shook her head. Lauren swayed, as if she were about to faint, but then caught herself and stood up ramrod straight. Kimberly's eyes got huge. KC smiled.

"Is this some kind of joke, Win?" Lauren finally asked.

Winnie shook her head. "No. Not at all," she said with great seriousness.

"This is no joke," Josh agreed.

Winnie held out her left hand and they saw a shiny gold band on one finger. "This is the ring Josh bought me there. You could even buy them pre-engraved with Elvis lyrics on them."

Faith reached out to touch the ring, as if that made all of this comprehensible. The others craned forward, too, but everybody looked a little scared, as if the ring might reach out and bite them.

"So anyway, that's it," Winnie summarized. "I know it was a long story and everything. And I know it sounds like the craziest thing to do."

Josh took over. "Maybe we didn't have bridesmaids and cakes and fancy flowers, but we love each other."

"And we're sure," Winnie promised, a tear in her throat.

Josh looked at the rest of them and smiled. "And we're married, forever more."

Josh kissed Winnie, which then turned into a crazy, we-know-this-is-nuts-but-we-love-each-other-so-much-we-don't-care laugh of deep, deep joy.

There was another huge laugh, and then everyone moved in for a big group hug.

Here's a sneak preview of
Freshman Promises, *the nineteenth*
book in the compelling story
of **FRESHMAN DORM.**

Winnie's mouth dropped open. The lobby of Lauren's former apartment house, where Winnie and Josh were living until the last few days of Lauren's lease ran out, looked as if it had been vandalized by some of the hoods who hung around the pawn shop at the end of the block.

Then, slowly, Winnie began to realize that the stuff heaped all over the filthy floor was—HERS!

Winnie gasped out loud at the mess. Smashed

at the bottom of the stairs were her precious Hawaiian paper lanterns covered with hula dancers. A cardboard box containing all of her high-school memorabilia, along with an assortment of poodle skirts, baseball hats, and Supergirl comic books, lay squashed and open in the middle of the floor. Poster tubes, dirty clothes, and the contents of their refrigerator were everywhere.

Not believing her eyes, Winnie waded through the strewn articles, picking some up and putting them aside. Then she flung off a sleeping bag that was draped over something huge near the stair railing. Her heart stopped. A massive motorcycle was underneath, gleaming in the dimly lit lobby. Winnie recognized the motorcycle as Peter Dvorsky's, but she couldn't fathom what it was doing there.

Faint sounds from above made her look up. She saw Josh emerge at the top of the first flight of stairs. He was moving backward slowly, dragging a large, plastic garbage bag.

"Josh!" Winnie cried out. "What happened?"

She watched him straighten up and turn to

look at her with a stony face. "It's moving day, Winnie," he snapped. "Remember?"

"But Josh, I thought we agreed that you would bring my hot-line banners to the Health Fair. I came back here because you didn't show."

Josh said not a word. Instead, he bent down to stuff junk that had scattered on the landing into the bag.

Winnie sighed. As a volunteer at the Crisis Hotline, she knew staying calm was the only way to get results. "Why don't you let me have the keys to the station wagon?" she said sensibly. "I'll drive the banners over myself."

"I can't, Winnie. I didn't buy the station wagon," Josh said, looking down at her and wiping his hands on the front of his torn sweatshirt. His pants were grimy, his eyes bloodshot, and he looked like he hadn't shaved in two days. "I bought Peter's motorcycle instead."

Winnie stood glued to the spot. Her lips began to quiver. "You what?"

"I bought Peter's bike."

Anger and indignation were beginning to

snake through Winnie's body. "You—you bought a motorcycle?" she whispered. "But I'm terrified of them."

"You are?" Josh twisted the top of the garbage bag and pulled a tie out of his back pocket. "You never told me that."

"A friend of mine in high school had a real bad accident on a bike. I was riding with him. I was just bruised, but he ended up with a ruptured spleen and spent months in the hospital. He could have died," Winnie said. She began to cry. "Couldn't you have asked me what I thought first? We're married now. We're supposed to consult each other before making big decisions. And we'd agreed to buy a car!"

Josh dropped the garbage bag and looked at her. His face was suddenly pale and drained. "So now you're feeling practical. Now you want to go the safe route," he shouted. "Well, just because you're the one who's in a jam this time, doesn't mean you can get your way. The other day you wanted to spend my parents' money on a hotel suite!"

"Keep it down out there," Mrs. Calvin yelled,

as she jerked open the door of her ground-floor apartment. "If you kids don't shut up and have all your stuff cleared out of here in an hour, I'll call the police!"

Josh ignored the landlady. He descended the stairs two at a time and his voice continued to rise with each step. "Did you ask me first before you dumped six hundred and fifty dollars on that shoebox of an apartment that doesn't even have a decent plug for a hot plate—much less for a computer?" he shouted.

Winnie stood there, speechless, as Josh approached her. He was really angry. She'd never seen him like this.

"Did you ask me before you ran off to the fair?" Josh went on. "Don't tell me you forgot that this was moving day?"

Tears were pouring down Winnie's cheeks. "Josh," she said softly. "Please!"

"Did you ask me before you decided to paint banners all week instead of packing your vast collection of junk? The new tenant is here, Winnie, just like Mrs. Calvin told us he would be. I couldn't move everything fast enough for her, so she personally threw your stuff down the stairwell to make room for him." He was standing right in front of her now, and he pointed at all that lay scattered about them. "Maybe you'd at least like to tell me what I should do with all of this?!"

A sob caught in Winnie's throat. *You're the one who ran off last night!* she thought, as she stared at Josh's angry face. He was turning into a stranger. And over what? A car? A bunch of stupid boxes they could have packed together last night if he hadn't run away?

Suddenly, Winnie saw red. Her whole body exploding with fury and sadness and frustration, she grabbed the plastic garbage bag from him and ripped off the tie.

"This is what you can do with my junk, Josh Gaffey," she yelled, dumping the bag upside down. A small hill of old Christmas cards, party hats, record-album covers and cheap paperbacks formed at his feet.

"And *this* . . ." Winnie picked up a broken blow dryer and threw it at Josh, narrowly missing his astonished head. Next she grabbed a box of Jell-O and sent it flying into his knee. "And this here!" she yelled, flinging an orange ankle boot into a dead potted plant. "I don't care what you do with this stuff. I don't care about *any* of it anymore! You can throw it all away. You can throw *me* away."

Tears streaming down her face, Winnie continued to hurtle things at Josh, as he slowly backed up toward his motorcycle. Everything was lost. Down the drain. She'd been wrong about him. "You can take these, too, and throw them away," Winnie sobbed, throwing her Rollerblades against the wall. *"You can throw our marriage away!"*

Josh's jaw clenched shut and he simply jerked the motorcycle around and started rolling it out the front door.

"Or you can stick our marriage vows on that deathmobile and crash the whole crazy idea into a brick wall!" Winnie cried.

She collapsed at the bottom of the stairs as she heard Josh rev up the engine and roar off.

"We'll never make this work," Winnie murmured, staring numbly at the battlefield before her. "It's too hard. It's just too hard."

Here's a peek at an exciting new book, First To Die, *A MOLLIE FOX MYSTERY by Peter Nelson*

*A*lthough she insisted nothing was wrong with her, Mollie agreed to let the school nurse look her over. Eva Fox went to call her husband to tell him the good news. Mollie was looking for the others, in a mob of brothers and sisters and friends, when she felt somebody tap her on the shoulder. She turned around to see Jordan, arms open and a big smile on his face.

"Mollie," he said. "I don't believe it. I mean, I believe it, because I told everyone you'd never let anything happen to you." He gave her a big hug. "I was so worried—I even went to the mall two nights to help dig, but there was just too much—I told them there were seven of you—what happened?"

Mollie reciprocated Jordan's hug halfheartedly. The sight of him with the blond girl hadn't exactly put her in a hugging mood.

"We got trapped in a tunnel," Mollie said. "The room we were in was completely destroyed, but we managed to make it into an old heating tunnel. It took us this long to dig our way out."

"You must be famished," Jordan said. "What was it like? Can I take you out for a cheeseburger or something?"

"We already ate. And it wasn't so bad, really. It was a little scary at first, but you can get used to just about anything."

"Listen to you, Miss Casual. I hope Johnny Chelios wasn't too much of a pain," Jordan said.

"Why do you say that?" Mollie said, her temper rising.

"I just mean, you know—everybody knows what a jerk he is."

"Be quiet, Jordan," Mollie said. "You don't know what you're talking about."

"Hey, I'm sorry," Jordan said.

"Johnny's my friend."

"Your friend," Jordan said. "What do you mean, friend?"

"I don't know," Mollie said. "Who's *your* friend, by the way? The blond girl I saw you holding hands with before I was even cold in the grave. You're lucky I didn't die, because that is why people get haunted, you know."

"Very funny," Jordan said.

"Sorry if I'm not laughing," Mollie said. "Look, Jordan, I'm just tired and I want to go home, so I'll see you later. Have fun with your friend."

"What?" Jordan said. "What blond girl? I didn't . . ." He struggled to recall. "Oh—hey, I can explain. You've got the wrong idea." He had a big smile on his face, the kind he got whenever he was feeling cocky, which Mollie knew Jordan equated in his own mind with being charming.

"Maybe some other time," Mollie said. "I just can't deal with much right now."

She saw her mother struggling to get away

from a television crew that wouldn't leave her alone. Sidestepping a reporter, Mollie hugged her mother again and whispered into her ear, "I just want to go home and take a shower and then come back to school—is that okay?"

"That's fine," Eva Doyle Fox said. "Your father was out of his mind with joy. He can't get away, but he wanted me to hug you for him. He's calling Donny. Rosemary's at day care, so I thought we'd stop by—she missed you so much."

Out of the corner of her eye, Mollie saw a lonely figure leaning against the end of the stage.

"Just a second, Mom," she said. "I have to go talk to somebody."

Johnny Chelios had his arms folded across his chest, amused at all the goings-on. So far no television or newspapper reporter had stuck a microphone in his face, and nobody had hugged him to welcome him back.

"Hey, buddy," Mollie said. "How you doing?"

"Great," Johnny said.

"I'm sorry," Mollie said. "I mean, about all the attention. . . ."

"Hell," Johnny said. "They didn't even know

I was down there. They only missed six people."

"You know what that means, don't you?" Mollie said.

"It means I don't exist."

"No," Mollie said. "It means neither Nick nor Benny went to the police, or else they would have known there were seven of us. It means those creeps left us for dead."

"Yeah," Johnny said. "Well, I know where Benny eats breakfast. He's usually there about noon. Maybe I'll go pay him a visit."

"Don't," Mollie said.

"Why not?"

"I mean, don't go without me," she said. She felt as if she were thinking clearly again. Maybe that was what they meant by food for thought. "We can't just walk up to him. We need some sort of plan."

"We? A plan for what?" Johnny said.

"I don't know," Mollie said. "Revenge is always good." Her mother gestured to her. "Where does Benny eat?"

"Dino's," Johnny said. "It's in the Brick District."

"I know it. I'll meet you in the parking lot there in an hour. Don't do anything without me, promise?"

"Promise," Johnny said. "Rat's honor." Mollie backed away. "Hey—what are you going to do with our friend?"

"Jordan?" Mollie said. "I don't know. Throw him off a bridge or something."

Johnny smiled. "Actually, the friend I meant is behind you."

Mollie looked to see Pirate sitting ten feet away, watching her and wagging his tail. Her mother saw the dog at the same time.

"Someone you know?" she asked.

"Yeah, Mom—this is Johnny Chelios. He was trapped with us."

"Nice to meet you, Johnny," Eva said, "but I was referring to the dog."

Mollie looked at her mom with pleading eyes. Pirate had taught her that trick.

"For the time being. Please, Mom?"

♣ HarperPaperbacks *By Mail*

Join KC, Faith, and Winnie as the three hometown friends share the triumphs, loves, and tragedies of their first year of college in this bestselling series:

FRESHMAN DORM

Away from home . . . and on their own!

KC Angeletti: Beautiful and talented, KC is a young woman on the move—and she'll do anything she can to succeed . . .

Winnie Gottlieb: Impulsive, reckless Winnie just can't keep her head on straight—how will she get through her first year?

Faith Crowley: Innocent Faith is Winnie and KC's best friend—but will she ever let loose and be her *own* friend?

Follow all the joys and heartaches of the girls of Freshman Dorm!